Lachlan

The MacGregors, Volume 3

Elina Emerald

Published by Elina Emerald, 2021.

LACHLAN

First edition. September 17, 2021.

Copyright © 2021 Elina Emerald.

ISBN: 979-8201504380

Written by Elina Emerald.

Table of Contents

To my ideal readers ...

Chapter 1

1048 Sadell Abbey, Argyll, Scotland

Two Months Earlier

"Where is Miriam Ferguson?" the warrior asked. His enormous hand with bloodied knuckles squeezed the abbess's neck with increased pressure.

The abbess remained indifferent, which was unusual behavior for someone in a precarious position. It was the quiet, assured confidence of a woman who felt no fear that the warrior posed any real threat.

She rasped through labored breaths, "If... you let... me speak... I'll... tell you."

The warrior pushed her away. She stumbled then righted herself, coughing as the air reentered her lungs. She rubbed her neck, knowing a bruise was already forming.

"Talk now!" he demanded in an abrasive tone.

"Miriam is here, but she is no longer with us," the abbess said between coughs.

"What do you mean?" he snarled, fist clenched.

The abbess pointed beyond the cloister to a small cemetery past the courtyard. A line of crosses framed the view. "Miriam rests among our dead."

"You lie!" he shouted. His hand shot out again. This time the abbess was prepared. She pulled her sgian-dubh from her sleeve. The sharp end of the blade now rested against his belly.

"I would think twice if I were you," she said. Her eyes held a steely glint.

He paused, dropped his arm, and stepped away.

The abbess stepped back, allowing more space between them. She retracted the blade. "I will ask you again, warrior, what did you want with Miriam?"

"She had something that belonged to my liege."

"All of Miriam's earthly possessions were distributed among the poor. There was nothing of value."

"What I seek is not material possession but something more, and I will find it with or without your help." He stepped forward again in a threatening manner but paused when he heard a quiet voice speak into the dimly lit cloister.

"Abbess Murdina, is everything well?" a woman asked. She stood a few feet away; her black hair was braided, and she wore a plain brown tunic. Her feet were bare. In her right hand, she casually leaned against a wooden quarterstaff. Anyone with a keen eye would notice she gripped it firmly, and she was not using it as a crutch.

The abbess exchanged a furtive glance, then replied, "All is well, Naomi. Our guest was just leaving."

The warrior briefly glanced at the newcomer. He noted she was a foreigner by her accent and complexion. He dismissed her and returned his gaze to the abbess.

"You think you can be rid of me that easily?" he asked rhetorically. "I ken you are hiding something within these walls, and I will find it even if I have to burn this abbey to the ground."

He grabbed the abbess by her arms, preparing to push her out of his way. But his action was interrupted when a wooden staff struck him hard on the side of the head. He released the abbess and turned toward the one called Naomi. His expression was one of confusion because the woman had not moved from her position, and she still leaned against the staff with an innocent expression on her face.

Not one to be fooled, he drew his sword only to find it flung out of his hands as Naomi rotated her staff with such speed and lashed out at his sword hand with a loud thwacking sound.

"Argh!" he snarled and gripped his injured hand. Before he could defend himself, Naomi took four steps, rotated the staff again, and struck him on the other side of the face.

"Bitch!" he yelled, stunned by the surprise attack. The warrior realized then he had made a grave error dismissing the foreigner so quickly. With his attention on her weapon, he failed to notice Naomi's foot moving towards his groin until it was too late. He stumbled to the floor in pain from the hard kick to his nether regions. When he raised his head to glare at her, all he saw was the quarterstaff aiming for his right temple.

"Cease!" the abbess shouted.

But it was too late. Naomi gripped the staff with both hands and side-swiped the warrior's temple. It knocked him out cold.

"By the saints, child. I told you I was all right!" the abbess scolded in frustration as she moved forward and crouched down to check on the warrior.

"He was going to hurt you," Naomi said while she was standing over the body, feet spaced apart, clutching her quarterstaff at a horizontal angle.

"Saints preserve us. Do you have so little faith in my abilities? Now he will be even more determined, you reckless gal." The abbess ranted while checking his pulse.

"Sorry, Abbess Murdina. I thought you were in danger," Naomi replied with a contrite expression.

"The only thing I'm in danger of is spending eternity in hell for teaching you to wield that thing."

Satisfied that the warrior still had a steady pulse, the abbess huffed, stood, and snatched the staff out of Naomi's hand. She propped it up against the wall and said, "You need to learn restraint. Violence is a last resort. Think before you act, lass."

"It will not happen again," Naomi replied.

The abbess sighed and said, "Lord kens, you will bring the wrath of the bishop upon us now. Come on then, help me move him."

Naomi reluctantly lifted the warrior's legs while the abbess lifted his upper body as they shuffled under his dead weight. Once they had placed him at the narthex, the abbess arranged for two laymen to move him out of the gates. Their task completed, the abbess locked the gates and barred the doors. The two women then moved to the cloister.

Naomi asked, "Abbess Murdina, what was he searching for?"

"Not what, who," she replied.

"Who was he searching for?" Naomi asked.

"Miriam."

Naomi gasped, "What did you tell him?"

"The same thing I tell anyone who seeks her."

"Then we must warn her," Naomi whispered.

The abbess shook her head and said, "No, we cannot lead them to her in any way. They are watching us, and more will come."

"But what about the ch—"

"Hush, lass! Dinnae speak of it here. The walls have ears," the abbess hissed as her eyes glanced about the inner courtyard.

Naomi remained silent then said, "Send me. I am fast. I can cover my tracks."

The abbess shook her head and whispered, "I require you here. Miriam kens the danger, and we have trained her well. We protect them all by staying the course."

"Aye, Abbess." Naomi nodded. She retrieved her staff. As Naomi followed the abbess down the dimly lit cloister, she sent up a silent prayer that the enemy never discovered the truth about Miriam Ferguson.

Present Day - Henderson Keep, Glencoe, Scotland

TYRA WALKED OUT THE door of the busy hall, leaving the festivities and abrupt noise behind her. She felt nauseated after the news she received from Sorcha. Lachlan was set to wed. Why did he not mention anything before?

She strode down the dimly lit passageway heading for the side entrance out of the Keep. She was practically gasping for air at the prospect that the man she had fallen in love with was soon to be married to someone else. For weeks, Tyra had hoped Lachlan would warm towards her, forgive her for the betrayal, but he remained cold and aloof. Now she realized why. He was courting someone else, and the thought pierced her heart with sadness. Now to make matters worse, Sorcha wanted Tyra to assist with the wedding feast. It was akin to pouring salt on a festering wound.

Tyra muttered to herself, "Why the bloody hell does he need my help?" The thought that she would have to witness Lachlan marry someone else, love someone else, was too much to bear.

"You're a damned fool," she said to no one. "As if he would have had any real interest in you."

"Who are you talking to?" Lachlan asked out of nowhere.

Tyra jumped in fright and almost came out of her skin. She paused with a hand on her chest to calm her racing heart.

"Sorry, I didnae mean to startle you," Lachlan said as he watched Tyra try to compose herself.

"Wha... what are you doing here? You scared the life out of me," she stammered as he hovered close by.

Lachlan moved even closer until he was towering over her. She strained her neck to peer up at him.

"I wanted to find out what you're doing out here in the dark," he replied.

Tyra tried not to stare too hard at his masculine jawline or the way his Adam's apple moved when he spoke.

"I... I was heading to my cottage."

"Alone?" he asked.

"Aye," Tyra replied.

"You're not sneaking off to tryst with that warrior I saw you with earlier tonight?"

"What warrior?"

"The one who was spinning you about with his hands all over you like a rash," Lachlan growled.

Tyra stepped back only to be backed against the wall. Lachlan moved forward, crowding her space.

"I dinnae ken what you speak of, Lachlan Gair. Now if you would please move, I can be on my way." She tried to move around him.

Lachlan stared at Tyra for some time but refused to move. The hallway was dimly lit, but there was enough light illuminating her features. His gaze landed on her lips, her full succulent lips, and he was mesmerized by them. He had stolen kisses from Tyra before, in another time and place when he thought she had genuine feelings for him. Standing this close to her again, Lachlan thought of only one thing as all sense left his brain.

"Lachie?" Tyra whispered in confusion. The dimples in her cheeks became prominent as she spoke.

"Damn you!" Lachlan growled and pulled her into his arms. Tyra gasped as his lips claimed hers. She could not think straight, and it was not long before she had her arms loosely wound about his shoulders as Lachlan deepened the kiss. All thought scattered to the four winds.

Lachlan pulled away first, breathing heavily as if trying to reason with himself. "Do you enjoy my kisses? Or are you pretending?" he asked but did not give her a chance to answer as his mouth sought hers once more.

Tyra pushed him back. She shook her head and said, "We canna do this. Not when you're promised to another."

Lachlan frowned. "What do you mean?"

"Dinnae trifle with me, Lachlan. You ken what I mean. You act like the injured party. Meanwhile, you have a betrothed you never mentioned." Tyra pushed him aside and tried to pass.

He pulled her back and asked, "Who told you that?"

"So, you admit it?" she accused.

"I admit nothing," he replied, exasperated.

"Dinnae play games with me, Lachlan Gair." Tyra was becoming increasingly agitated.

"So, is this what you do? Flash your pretty dimples and toy with men."

"My dimples? What has that got to do with anything?"

"You are a liar, Tyra Henderson, and I will not be led by the nose." Lachlan glowered at her.

Tyra felt as if he had struck her with his open palm. She flinched and stepped back. "I'm the liar now? When you're the one who has misrepresented yourself."

They were both glaring at each other in silence when someone cleared their throat nearby.

Lachlan immediately released Tyra as if she was a bag of hot coals. He turned to see Kieran standing a few feet away.

"Lach, sorry to bother you, but Bram wants a word," Kieran said.

"Aye, I'll be there directly," Lachlan replied, then returned his gaze to Tyra and said, "Dinnae walk at night alone. I cannot stop you from sneaking about with other men, but you will remain safe."

"I dinnae sneak about with men!" she hissed in protest.

"I dinnae care what you do," Lachlan bit out in return. He stepped away from her in a dismissive manner. As he walked past Kieran, he said, "See Tyra home."

"Aye," Kieran replied.

Lachlan proceeded down the hall without a second glance.

"What a turd," Tyra muttered under her breath, frantically trying to smooth her hair.

Kieran just chuckled. "An angry turd by the look of it."

"Does he always behave like an ogre?" she asked Kieran.

"Only where you're concerned, lass," he replied. "C'mon, I best get you home before the turd returns."

As they began walking, Tyra asked, "What did Bram want with Lachlan?"

"Something about a woman."

"What woman?" Tyra asked.

"I didnae ask." Kieran shrugged his shoulders.

Tyra wanted to return to the hall and find out who this woman was. But she mentally shook her head. No, she was not going to do that. It was most likely Lachlan's bride-to-be. She was fuming that he would kiss her when he was betrothed to be married. Men were such fickle creatures, she thought.

In the Light of Day

LACHLAN OPENED HIS eyes the following morning and immediately regretted it. The light streamed through the small window slit in his room, and it was enough to burn a hole in his retina. He squinted, then shut his eyes again and brought a hand to his forehead to block out the glare. His head pounded, he felt parched, and he was partly mind-fogged. He could barely recollect the previous evening's activities as he peered at the rafters above.

Lachlan groaned and sat up slowly. The room spun with a sudden rush of blood to the head. He gripped the bedding, flung his legs over the side, and just sat and contemplated the sorry state of his life. His prominent thought was that he really needed to stop drinking because he was getting too old for it. Lachlan felt a stinging pain in his chest. He instinctively rubbed it. It was not physical pain, more like the familiar empty feeling he experienced whenever he nursed a broken heart. He closed his eyes, and his mind conjured up images of a dimpled smile, sandy hair, and hazel-colored eyes.

Tyra Henderson, that's who he thought about first thing in the morning and the last thing at night. He partially smiled as he recalled how soft her lips were the night before when he had followed her out of the hall. She was a beauty, a gentle soul with a hard edge, but it was her scent of honeysuckle he loved the most. Lachlan felt the cavity in his chest fill slightly with warmth, then dissipate when he recalled the harsh words and his callous actions that caused her stricken expression. He could be a bastard when he wanted to, but betrayal was a bitter pill to swallow, and he had his fair share.

Tyra had pretended to like him and distracted him so Bram Henderson could kidnap Sorcha MacGregor while Lachlan was meant to be guarding her. He cringed at the memory of his failure. Even though it all ended well, and Bram eventually married Sorcha, Lachlan could no longer trust his judgment when it came to the opposite sex.

He grumbled to himself. Lachlan saw the pitcher on the mantle and decided it was time to get out of bed, wash, and stop these maudlin thoughts. He was about to rise when he felt the bed shift slightly. Lachlan's spine tingled, and his back went rigid. He whipped his head to the side, and he sucked in a breath. A shapely bared thigh rested there. He looked at the body attached to the shapely thigh and practically jumped off the bed. He paled.

What the bloody hell?

Lachlan immediately stepped back, trying to put as much distance between him and the semi-dressed woman currently asleep on her stomach in his bed. Her tresses had come loose as waves of abundant curls danced across her back.

He looked down at his body. His trews were still intact, although riding low on his hips. Events from the night before were murky at best. He remembered meeting Bram about some woman, and then Iain and Niall poured him a drink or a hundred. He could not remember because the rest was a blur. One thing was certain: he had imbibed more than was healthy. Either way, Lachlan realized this turn of events was not good, and she needed to leave.

Shite! He cursed to himself. Not only would Beiste MacGregor beat him to a pulp, but Ruadh MacDonald would also belt him within an inch of his life if she was discovered in Lachlan's bed. In his panic, Lachlan thought of Tyra. For some inextricable reason, he wondered what she would think of him. He inched closer towards the bed and gently nudged the woman to wake her. She grumbled and turned her head the other way.

"Lass! You canna be caught in here. Wake up!" he urged.

He kept on nudging her shoulder with his hand until finally, she huffed and sat up.

"All right! I am awake. No need to be annoying."

"I'm annoying? What are you doing in my bed?" Lachlan scowled.

"Well, what does it bloody well look like?" she replied.

"Did we... Did we couple yestereve?" Lachlan paled and held his breath, waiting for her response. Surely, he would remember something like that. How much had he imbibed? He wondered.

"How can you not remember the best night of your life?" she asked and gave him an insulted look. "I am offended you dinnae recollect how I brought you to the heights of ecstasy several times. Not to mention what you did to me." She winked.

Lachlan felt his lungs constrict. No, it could not be. He rubbed his chest in panic and pain. If he had indeed engaged in a drunken tryst, he would have to marry her. A million thoughts flew through his head, the most pressing being one of sheer panic and a need to vomit.

The woman in question began giggling. "Oh, the look on your face tis so amusing!" She laughed and clapped her hands. "Dinnae fash yourself, I was merely trifling with you. Please breathe before you pass out."

Lachlan stared at her with a frown as sheer relief coursed through his veins. "What are you playing at? And why are you here?"

"Tsk, you take life far too seriously. We did not couple, and you can wipe that grimace from your face. You look as if you bedded a wilder beast." She got out of bed and straightened her chemise. "Truth be told, you were very drunk, which serves you right when you take on the Hendersons in a drinking contest you are bound to lose."

Lachlan felt pure relief at her admission.

"Then what the hell are you doing in my room?" Lachlan asked in confusion.

Yesenda MacDonald casually tied back her hair with a hair tie and replied, "I needed somewhere safe to hide, and your door was unlocked. I must have fallen asleep, which is a miracle considering how loud you snore."

"I dinnae snore," Lachlan replied defensively. Yesenda just rolled her eyes and walked towards the pitcher of water as if she owned the room.

"Why did you hide in here? Are you daft? You should not avail yourself of men's living quarters." Lachlan found his leine and quickly donned it while refastening his trews.

"You sound like the abbess with all your outrage. Calm yourself. I will leave shortly." Yesenda picked up a cloth, wiped her face, walked over to the side of the bed, and started dressing.

Lachlan couldn't believe how casually she strode about the room without a care in the world. "Do you ken what would happen if you were found in my room? You need to go now," he grumbled.

"Wheesht, keep your voice down. Help me fasten my kirtle."

Yesenda turned her back to Lachlan, her hands behind her, holding the ties' ends for him to take the reins. "Go on, hurry up if you want me gone."

"Bloody hell, I am not a lady's maid," Lachlan scowled as he complied.

Yesenda chuckled and turned her head to look behind her, saying, "Tis a pity. You would make such a bonnie lady with your high cheekbones and fine eyes."

Lachlan just glared at her and deliberately tightened her stays.

"Ouch!" Yesenda said as he fastened it too tight. "Well, I can see you are a man who does not favor the mornings."

"What I dinnae favor is finding a strange woman in my bed whose brother could kill me for the slight."

Yesenda just shrugged. Once she was ready, Lachlan moved to the door to check outside, making sure the coast was clear. He ushered her towards it. Lachlan paused when a thought occurred to him. "Why were you in danger?" he asked.

"Twas nothing. I just heard something that spooked me a little. My nerves are slightly frayed when I am in a strange place." She brushed it off.

Lachlan did not quite believe her, but noises from the hallway urged him to remove her from his room. "Very well. If you are in danger again, at least wake me up first, so I am not startled in the morn by your unwelcome presence."

Yesenda smirked and replied, "Why, how romantic you are, Lachlan Gair. Women must swoon at your words of adoration." She raised her airisaidh over her head to conceal her identity then quit the room.

Lachlan could just make out her profile disappearing down one of the passageways, then she was gone. He closed the door and scratched his head, baffled at what had just transpired and at the ease with which

Yesenda carried herself as if she had done this 'hiding' thing many times before. He made a mental note that he would keep a closer eye on her.

Lachlan put Yesenda out of his mind and washed with the remaining water in a barrel. He focused on the day ahead. As a guardsman, he had much to do.

Chapter 2

The Longhouse – Glencoe Valley

Tyra stripped off her clothes and plunged headfirst into the freezing water. She emerged moments later, shivering, then proceeded to scrub herself with the lavender soap. Her teeth were chattering, but her body became accustomed to the cold as Tyra washed some more. She waded closer to the riverbank and was now waist-deep and rinsing the soap from her skin. It was a secluded spot just downstream from her cottage. It was first light when the weather was coldest, but after a restless night obsessing over Lachlan and that kiss, Tyra needed something like this to wake her up and snap her out of her current mood.

Tyra paused when she heard a rustling sound. She grabbed a large rock from the riverbed and held it tight in her fist. She scanned her surroundings when a pheasant walked out from the shrubbery.

"Stupid bird," she hissed, then burst out laughing with relief. She dropped the rock, finished her bath, then dried off and changed into her garments behind a hedge of trees.

When she was fully clothed, Tyra felt the odd sensation of being watched. She whipped her head around and pulled her dirk out as she scanned the woods again. But there was nothing. Resigned that it must be in her mind, she quickly headed to the longhouse to prepare breakfast for herself and Iain. It was just the two of them now who remained in the row of white cottages.

Fia and her grandchildren—Mysie, Domhnall, and Michael—had moved to the Keep with Bram and Sorcha Henderson. Niall, Bram's brother, moved to the warrior's quarters, and Willa, Bram's sister, and Willa's toddler, Inan, moved to a cottage closer to the Keep. It was a good arrangement as the children spent most of their time with Sorcha and Fia. They were safer in the bosom of the clan than out in the glen.

Tyra preferred the quiet of the glen and now used the longhouse as her healer's cottage while she lived in the house next door. Iain also chose to remain in his own home, which was a short walk away. He preferred the quiet to noisy Keep life, but he was always on hand whenever Bram needed him.

Iain and Tyra still shared breakfast together in the mornings. It was a tradition Tyra enjoyed as there were few times she had to just talk with her brother. But especially today, she wanted to pry information from Iain about what happened in the hall after she left.

As Tyra neared the longhouse, she could smell a delicious aroma of fresh meat frying on the pan and bread baking. Her stomach grumbled, and she realized she was famished. Tyra was surprised Iain was up so early cooking, but she was too hungry to second guess it. She opened the door with a huge smile, and it died instantly when she realized Iain was not alone.

Tyra clenched her jaw when she saw his companion sitting at the table without a care in the world while Iain prepared the meal over the woodfire.

"Tyra! Tis lovely to see you. We are just about to break our fast," the woman said.

"What are you doing here, Lìosa?" Tyra asked.

"Dinnae be rude, Tyra." Iain gave her a warning glare.

Lìosa seemed oblivious to the tension between the siblings. "I am here because I missed my darling, Iain."

Iain moved to the bench with the hot pan and served up food portions on his prepared trenchers. "Come and eat while it's still hot.

The bread is freshly baked," he said, giving Tyra a silent warning to be polite to his on-again-off-again lover.

Tyra begrudgingly stomped towards the table and took a stool on the opposite side. She grabbed a knife and began slicing the bread. "Did you bake this?" she asked Lìosa.

"You ken I dinnae cook. Tis all Iain. He spoils me." Lìosa gave Iain a sultry smile and kissed his cheek when he sat down to eat.

Iain just blushed and said, "Let me say the grace."

Tyra bowed her head, and Iain said the blessing. "Lord, thank you for your bountiful provisions and for kin to share a warm meal, Amen."

"Amen," Tyra responded. Then she poured them all fresh cider.

Lìosa smirked. "Iain, you are so serious with your prayerful ways. You should have been a monk."

Iain shrugged and replied, "Tis important to give thanks, Lìosa. We never ken when we will eat again. Gratitude keeps us humble."

"Aye, some of us still ken what it's like to go without," Tyra said, remembering that life under the old laird had been hard on the crofters and clan.

Iain just nodded.

There was silence before they started eating. The food was delicious, but Tyra wished Lìosa Haxton was not there. Lìosa was Iain's childhood sweetheart, and a woman Tyra despised because she knew Iain deserved much better than a woman who came and went without warning.

In an attempt to change the subject, Lìosa said, "My love, I thought it would be nice to visit the Keep today. It has been an age since I've seen old friends. Mayhap we could wander through the markets afterward. You could get me that keepsake you mentioned?"

"Keepsake?" Tyra asked.

"A silver ring Iain wanted to buy me. You remember, Iain?"

"Aye, I remember, Lìosa. You were not keen on it before. Said it was not to your liking," Iain replied.

"I said no such thing! I just didnae want you wasting precious coin on me."

Iain remained silent and kept chewing.

Tyra felt the tension coming from the other side of the table. She asked, "So how long are you here for this time, Lìosa? A sennight? A day? Or will you be hying off to your wealthy merchant once you've eaten all our food?"

"Tyra!" Iain growled.

Tyra just resumed eating.

Lìosa replied in a sweet voice, "Tis all right, my love. I ken we are all old acquaintances here. Dinnae be angry with your sister on my behalf, my darling. You are so braw when you get riled."

Tyra wanted to throw up her breakfast at the sickly display of affection. Not for the first time, she wondered how Iain could continue to favor a woman who was all pretense.

Lìosa turned towards Tyra and answered, "I will be here a sennight to visit with my kin, then I have matters in Yorkshire to attend to."

It was Iain's turn to tense up. "You didnae tell me that when you arrived."

"Darling, of course, I did. You were obviously too enamored to pay attention." Lìosa winked at him.

There was silence between them again.

"What do you have to do in Yorkshire? Mayhap I can accompany you?" Iain asked nonchalantly, glancing at Lìosa.

Lìosa paled slightly then disguised it. "Dinnae fash, tis just some kin matter."

Silence ensued before Iain asked, "Is there a wealthy man waiting for you there?"

"Good lord, Iain, what has gotten into you? You ken I dinnae have anyone else?" Lìosa tucked her arm under Iain's and said, "Darling, tis me, your rùnag?" She caressed his cheek with the back of her hand.

Tyra watched the exchange and noticed something different in Iain's response. Usually, Lìosa just needed to bat her lashes, and that was enough to appease Iain. But this time, Tyra caught a flash of something else in Iain's eyes. Irritation. It was a new look for him, an expression he'd never directed towards Lìosa before. Even Lìosa seemed surprised by it.

Tyra grinned secretly as she dug into her food with gusto, her appetite returning with the knowledge that there was hope for her brother after all.

Sneaking About

AFTER BREAKING HER fast, Tyra gathered her wool basket and made her way to the Keep to join the weaving circle for a couple of hours. The women now had a large room where they gathered to treat the wool and weave the plaid. She touched her lips when she remembered Lachlan's kiss from the previous night. For a brief moment, Lachlan had set aside his disdain for her, and he had kissed her with abandon. Tyra thought it was a languid, honeyed kiss, and she was sad it had ended the way it did. She sighed with the knowledge that he would soon be married, and she really had no business kissing betrothed men.

Tyra was just moving down the hallway when she saw Lachlan's bedchamber door opening. She faltered when she observed a woman slip out of the room. Her heart sank right to the bottom of the sea. To think that she still remembered the searing kiss. Clearly, it was not as memorable for him.

Tyra turned her eyes downcast upon the floor. To think the big lout followed her out of the hall then kissed her senseless only to then fall into the arms of another woman. It was too much to bear. Tyra was angry because Lachlan had accused her of playing games, and yet there he was a mere hours later entertaining his lover. She just shook her head. She was done dreaming about Lachlan like a love-sick fool. Enough was enough.

Tyra continued to the weaving room and put all thoughts of Lachlan out of her mind. When she rounded the corner, she saw Amelia and Beiste MacGregor locked in an intimate embrace. Their faces were inches apart, and they were whispering as lovers do. Tyra envied their relationship. Even after several years of marriage and four boisterous children, the Beast of the Highlands was still besotted with his wife. They were known to tryst in secret places around the Keep and swim together naked in the river when their bairns were abed.

Chieftain Beiste MacGregor was Sorcha Henderson's brother. His wife Amelia was a reputed healer, and the MacGregors were visiting Henderson Keep so Amelia could provide Sorcha with medical assistance during her pregnancy.

Tyra quietly retraced her steps so as not to disturb the couple. She wondered what it would be like to have a man that devoted to her well-being as Beiste was to Amelia. Her smile disappeared as she contemplated the bleak future ahead. There was no way she would find such a man.

Weavers Circle

TYRA NODDED AT CONNOR, the guardsman, then entered the large room. It was noisy with women chatting as they worked.

"Morning, Tyra," Fia greeted as several other women followed.

"Good morn, ladies," she replied and sat down beside Fia to begin her task. She preferred to work quietly and just listen to the gossip as the women chatted continuously around her.

"I heard the MacGregors are leaving soon. I must say I'll miss the wee ones running aboot the Keep and squealing with laughter," Blair said. She was a crofter's wife and one of the regular weavers.

"Aye, they're a mischievous bunch but good-hearted, especially the older lads. They keep the young-uns in line," Esme piped in. She was the eldest of all the weavers, and her skill was exceptional.

"'Tis the bonnie wee lasses who'll be keeping their das on their toes for years to come. Just the other day, I caught them climbing the trees trying to shoot things with their bows and arrows," Blair said.

"I hear they gave Duff Henderson the fright of his life when his hat got knocked clean off his head," Esme added.

"Were they aiming for his head?" someone asked.

"No, they were aiming for a tree trunk. Duff just happened to walk by at the wrong time and och the blather that went on about how the sidhe tried to attack him in the forest."

The women burst out laughing.

Blair replied, "Serves him right to be frightened for a change. He is always scaring the bairns about brownies in the woods."

The women continued chatting.

"I thought the MacGregors were staying until Sorcha's babe is born?" Tyra whispered to Fia and Willa.

"No, there are matters in Glenorchy the men must attend to. Amelia wanted to stay, but Beiste will not leave his wife behind," Fia replied.

"Aye, they had a huge row over it last night. I've never heard a woman raise her voice to a chieftain before. It was something to behold," Willa said.

"I take it Beiste won?" Tyra asked.

"Hardly, he did a lot of bellowing himself, then the fighting ceased, and the rutting began," Willa replied.

"What?" Tyra asked with a scandalized expression.

Willa huddled closer and whispered, "Aye, suddenly nothing but moaning sounds were coming from their chamber, and then this morn, Amelia announced they were leaving soon, but she will return closer to Sorcha's lying in." Willa grinned and just shook her head.

Fia chuckled and said, "Amelia won in the end. Twas what she really wanted to begin with."

Tyra became distracted when the other women started discussing Lachlan.

"That braw one, Lachlan, and his friend Kieran, I hear they are to remain with our clan a wee bit longer. Chieftain MacGregor insists they guard our mistress for an extra year."

"Lachlan is verra handsome. Do you ken if he is spoken for?" one of the younger women asked.

"Word is, he is aboot to wed a bonnie lass from the village. The laird and mistress ken all about it," Blair replied.

"Och, tis a pity because I was hoping to warm his bed for the year," another woman joked as the group burst into a fit of giggles.

"Who is the woman?" Tyra asked.

Blair replied, "Tis a mystery. They have been courting in secret for several months. It must be true love."

Tyra just paled and refocused on her task, blocking out all the other chatter.

Chapter 3

Cursed

Lachlan was cursed, and he knew it. He had spent the past two days doing all in his power to avoid Tyra Henderson, but the universe kept conspiring against him. He knew he needed to keep his distance from her, especially after that delectable kiss in the hallway, but every time he tried, Sorcha would send him on an errand that would put him directly in Tyra's path.

The more time Lachlan spent in Tyra's presence, the more he wanted her. As his craving increased, so did his anger. His only line of defense was to give her death stares so she would stay away from him because, Lord help him, Lachlan's resolve was weakening.

"Why did I have such terrible luck with women?" he wondered, not for the first time.

First, there was his childhood sweetheart, Heather, who dealt him a crushing blow by running off with his best friend on what was supposed to be their wedding day. Then there was Elora, who was involved in a plot to harm Amelia MacGregor. She was now languishing in a prison cell at Macbeth's Castle in Dunsinane. There had been no one since... until Tyra. She was different. He felt an instant connection from the moment he laid eyes on her, and he hoped like hell she felt the same way. Like winter thaws into spring, he felt the icy cold compression ease with Tyra's sunny disposition. He loved talking to her, and he rarely spoke that long with any woman. But with Tyra, he felt like he could tell her everything.

Turns out it was all a ruse.

"You stupid imbecile!" he muttered to himself as he strode through the tall grass to fetch Tyra from the marshes. His breath caught when he came to a clearing, and the object of his affection and disdain appeared. She was picking sundew. She was beautiful, he thought. A beautiful, treacherous liar.

Lachlan watched her scooping the plants into a basket with gentle concentration. When she tilted her head in his direction, Lachlan bit his lip to keep from groaning. She was sublime even from her side profile. She had a firm, voluptuous figure and a narrow waist that flared out to rounded hips. He still wanted her, and that's why he needed to keep his distance.

"Tyra!" he snapped as he walked towards her.

She stopped what she was doing. "Aye?" she asked with a raised brow.

"Sorcha said there are warriors who need tending to at the Keep. I'm here to escort you back."

Tyra nodded. "Thank you for the message. I'll be there shortly." She turned back to her task, dismissing him instantly.

Lachlan wanted her eyes on him, and he was smarting from how easily she dismissed him. Without thinking, he snatched the basket away from her and said, "No, you will come with me now. I dinnae have time to wait around for you."

Tyra got to her feet in an instant and said, "Give me back my basket." She reached across to try and pry it from his fingers, but Lachlan lifted it high so it was out of her reach. Given he was much taller, Tyra tried to jump up and grab it, and Lachlan kept moving it away. Each time her body brushed up against his, he gritted his teeth.

"Cease jumping. It will do you no good."

Tyra eventually stopped and stepped away from him. "I dinnae ken why you have to be such an ass about this."

Lachlan just gritted his teeth. "Dinnae think I enjoy chasing you about. Tis Beiste's orders that I remain here for another year to guard Sorcha, and unfortunately, with Sorcha comes you."

"I'm so sorry my presence displeases you so much, but I can walk to the Keep by myself. Hand me my basket!" Tyra demanded with her outstretched arm and open palm.

Lachlan was not sure why he was making an issue of the basket, but he felt the need to taunt her, so he said, "If you want it, you can pry it from my cold dead fingers."

Tyra glared at him then said, "Very well. If you want to behave like a bampot, so be it."

She walked a few feet away, stooped down, and picked up a clump of mud. She turned back towards Lachlan and hurled it with all her might at his face.

Lachlan dodged the flying missile, but it splattered across his shoulder. He looked down to see his pristine white leine now stained with mud. By the time he glanced back up again, Tyra was already storming back to the Keep.

"Why, you hellion, this is my favorite garment!" he shouted.

Tyra stuck her tongue out at him. "Go boil your head, you bawsack!"

Lachlan was livid. It was his favorite leine. No woman had ever thrown mud at his face before and then called him a bawsack. Lachlan dropped the basket on the ground and roared, "Come back here!"

Tyra turned around just in time to see Lachlan charging towards her like an enraged bull. She screamed, turned on her heel, and ran for the Keep. Hysteria and adrenaline combined to give her speed, but he closed the distance so fast. Within a matter of moments, Tyra found herself tackled to the ground from behind.

Lachlan twisted in time so he hit the ground first, landing on his back; he cushioned Tyra's fall. When she lay above him, his arms locked around her as he held her tightly against him. Their faces were inches apart, and both were breathing heavily.

With their bodies fused together, Lachlan realized he had made a monumental mistake. Suddenly, anger and ire were replaced by something altogether different as his body responded to having Tyra pressed up against him. He cursed and willed himself not to become aroused, but his secret was already out.

Tyra was not immune to the same feelings as her breathing became shallow and her nipples hardened with the intimate position of their bodies. When she felt Lachlan's arousal nudging against her thigh, she stilled and stared straight into his eyes. The fire was banked, and Tyra felt a burning passion searing her soul. She knew Lachlan still had feelings for her.

Blanking out all other thoughts, her eyes softened, and before she could think better of it, Tyra leaned closer and touched her lips to his. Lachlan groaned. He rolled over and shifted their position so he now hovered above her, and he deepened the kiss as his hands caressed her body. The feel and scent of her set his heart racing. He wanted nothing more than to lift her skirts and satisfy his craving deep within her.

"Open!" he growled.

Tyra opened her mouth slightly, and Lachlan's tongue caressed hers. They remained locked in an intimate embrace, oblivious to their surroundings. Nothing existed except their touch.

"Lachie," Tyra moaned against his lips as she tried to take a breath.

The use of his pet name brought Lachlan to his senses. He remembered she'd called him that several times when they met in the woods at Glenorchy. When she lied to him. Lachlan stilled and pulled away from her.

"Damn it to hell," he cursed.

"What's wrong?" Tyra sat up, frowning.

"You. You're what's wrong. Everything about you is wrong. I canna kiss a woman whose lips speak falsehoods so easily." He grumbled as he got to his feet. Lachlan tried not to flinch when he saw the stricken expression on her face.

Tyra made to stand, and Lachlan reached down to help her up, but she slapped his hand away. "Dinnae touch me!" she hissed. "And I assure you, that is the last kiss you ever steal from these lips."

She stood, straightened her clothing, and refused to look at him. On the verge of tears, she turned on her heel and strode back towards the Keep. Lachlan immediately followed close behind. He tried to think of something to say, but the anger coming off her was palpable.

Then Tyra stopped abruptly, turned to face him, and unleashed: "I have apologized several times for what happened with Sorcha. I may have lied so Bram could steal her away, but my feelings for you were genuine. Twas no lie. Yet you treat me like vermin every chance you get. Well, have at it, Lachlan Gair. I am done with you too because you are wrong for me as well!" She kept walking, then stopped, faced him again, and drove the last nail straight into his coffin when she said, "And someday when I find a man worthy of my love, I'll thank the Lord above that he is not you!" With those parting words, Tyra held her head high and her spine straight as a plumb line and left him behind.

Lachlan felt the direct hit of her words as if she had punctured his lung. He thought about the last part of her line. The thought of her with any other man did not sit well with him, which just worsened his mood. He watched Tyra march up to the Keep, and he was tempted to drag her back and ensure no other man claimed her. But he dug his fingers into his palms to keep from reaching out for her again.

As Lachlan watched Tyra walk away, he could not help but still admire her. He thought it interesting how much she resembled Yesenda MacDonald from behind. If one did not see her face, she could easily be mistaken for Yesenda. He shook his head at the random thought, and after a deep sigh, he reluctantly followed.

The Ambush

THE FOLLOWING DAY, Lachlan answered the summons that Sorcha wanted to see him in her solar. When he entered the room, he saw Bram Henderson sitting beside his wife. Bram looked reluctant to be there, and Lachlan knew immediately it was an ambush. Sorcha had a glint in her eye, which meant she had called her husband for backup, and the besotted fool was going to stand by whatever daft decision Sorcha was about to make concerning him. Lachlan braced himself for some major unpleasantness.

Bram sat beside Sorcha, looking every inch the smitten husband while Sorcha hand-sewed a tiny garment for their unborn babe. Her stomach had increased exponentially; she could rest her arms on her belly.

"You wanted to see me?" Lachlan asked.

"Aye, I've called you here because I think tis time you married and settled down," Sorcha replied.

"Are you daft?" Lachlan was genuinely shocked by Sorcha's comment.

Sorcha sewed a couple of stitches then said, "I am all seriousness. I am concerned about you, Lachlan. You're not getting any younger, and I dinnae want you turning into grumpy old man Menzie."

"Colm Menzie is close to a hundred years old, Sorcha."

"Aye, and when he was your age, he didnae bother finding a wife, and look what happened... he is now a bitter, lonely man sitting on that hill throwing rocks at strangers," Sorcha replied.

"With respect, Sorcha, tis none of your concern what happens to me," Lachlan said. "And there's nothing wrong with throwing rocks at strangers."

"Aye love, leave him be," Bram said.

Sorcha ignored Bram and continued, "Be that as it may, I have found the perfect woman for you. She is unattached and in need of a good man to wed."

Lachlan replied, "Then she can remain unattached, because I am not a good man."

Changing tack, Sorcha glanced at Bram and nudged him in the ribs. Bram subtly shook his head and mouthed, "No." Sorcha pinched Bram on the thigh, and again he mouthed, "No."

Sorcha glared at Bram, and she reached across to pinch him again. Bram moved his thigh out of the way, sighed, and said, "Lachlan, please just consider my wife's proposal."

"With respect, Laird Henderson, I dinnae want to meet whatever woman your wife has dredged up from the bog pit."

"She is not from the bog pit!" Sorcha replied, outraged.

"Regardless, I am still a retainer for the MacGregor chieftain, and I am not at liberty to wed at will."

"Nonsense. Beiste would not care if you took a wife," Sorcha replied.

Lachlan gritted his teeth and said, "Be that as it may, I dinnae ken why you feel the need to take charge of my life."

Bram said, "Lachlan, I have been married to a MacGregor for a short time, and I ken your clanswomen are a stubborn lot when they get a daft notion in their heads, so you might as well agree."

"Aye, Lachlan, you will see the right of it too. You need the touch of a good woman," Sorcha added.

"I've been touched by plenty of women, and I can tell you they're not worth it," Lachlan replied.

Bram chuckled at Lachlan's comment, and Sorcha elbowed him in the ribs.

"Is this about Elora?" Sorcha asked. "None of that was your fault. No one kenned she was in cahoots with Ludan."

Lachlan replied, "Tis not about Elora. Tis about women in general. They lie, and I canna abide by it."

"This is about Tyra, then? C'mon Lachlan, surely you cannot still be angry with her?" Sorcha asked rhetorically. "If it were not for Tyra,

I would not have met my beloved Bram, and as you can see, all has turned out well for us." Sorcha gestured to her large baby bump.

"Felicitations to you both then," Lachlan snorted with sarcasm.

They were interrupted when Tyra entered the room. She had her head turned behind her while she talked to a warrior named Dermid. He was carrying a heavy basket of clothes. He said something to Tyra, and she giggled. Tyra had not realized the others were in the room until she turned and stilled when Lachlan glared at her.

Dermid kept grinning and said, "Pardon me, we did not ken anyone was in here. I was just helping Tyra with these."

"Tis all right, Dermid, just leave the things and go," Bram replied.

Dermid nodded, quickly placed the basket to the side, then quit the room. He was unperturbed even as Lachlan gave him a death stare.

"I can come back later..." Tyra said.

"Tis alright, cousin, come and take a seat. Thank you for bringing my things. We were all just discussing something with Lachlan," Sorcha said and ushered Tyra to sit in the empty chair beside him.

Lachlan continued to glare at Tyra with a cold accusatory stare, and she reluctantly sat down.

Lachlan muttered under his breath, "Has Dermid stolen kisses from you?"

Tyra snapped, "What do you care?"

Lachlan glowered at her then said, "Sorcha! You're right. Tis time I wed. I trust you to arrange it."

Sorcha and Bram looked surprised at the sudden announcement.

"Of course, I shall make the arrangements," Sorcha replied.

"Good. If we're finished here, I need to see to my duties," Lachlan said.

"Wait, there's one more thing before you go," Sorcha said. She put her sewing down.

"What is it?"

"Tyra is going to help you plan the wedding."

"She is?" Bram asked Sorcha, looking confused. Sorcha kicked Bram under the table, and he said, "Oh aye, Tyra will help you... ah... plan," Bram said.

Tyra interrupted, "I think tis best Lachlan and his bride do their own planning. I dinnae have the time."

"I agree. I would not want to take up Tyra's precious time, what with her hands being full of warriors," Lachlan replied.

Tyra whipped her head around and hissed at Lachlan, "Take that back!"

"I speak as I find," he murmured in return.

She squinted her eyes, digging her nails into her palm to refrain from slapping him across the face. "I pity your new bride. She must be daft to put up with you."

"At least she's not a liar," he muttered.

"At least I'm not a donkey's ass," she replied.

The two of them remained in a stare-off as Sorcha and Bram watched the exchange, not quite knowing what to do. Fortunately, Sorcha's sisters-in-law Amelia MacGregor, Zala Fletcher, and Clarissa Robertson arrived to break the stalemate. They entered the solar with a loud cacophony of noisy bairns following close behind.

"Here you all are! I wondered where you got to. Sorcha, I have some things for the babe," Amelia said, waving a basket of clothes in the air. "Tyra, I will come and see you at the longhouse after the noonday meal if that suits you? I have some remedies to give you and further instructions before we leave."

Tyra replied, "I would very much appreciate your wisdom, Amelia."

Amelia beamed at her. She had been teaching Tyra a vast array of healing methods for different ailments and preparing her for anything should Sorcha need help during her pregnancy.

Zala said, "Bram, Iain and Niall are searching for you. They were in the main hall."

Clarissa added, "And Lachlan, Beiste, Brodie, and Dalziel were looking for you. They are also in the main hall."

The women issued orders to their children, who all complied and took seats by the window where they quietly kept each other company.

Bram stood and replied, "Thank you, ladies. Lachlan and I will head to the hall now." He stooped down and gave Sorcha a searing kiss which made her blush. Then he took his leave.

As the men left the women and children in the solar, Lachlan gave Tyra scathing looks on the way out. Tyra just muttered, "Coo dung," under her breath, then turned her attention to the new arrivals.

"What was that all about?" Zala asked.

"I've never seen Lachlan in such a feral mood. He's usually all smiles," Amelia said.

"Did we interrupt something?" Clarissa asked.

Sorcha subtly shook her head. It was a signal for her sisters to drop the subject, so they did.

Then Sorcha asked, "Sisters, do you mind if I have a private word with Tyra, and I'll be with you shortly?"

"Not at all," Clarissa replied with a smile.

When the women had moved to the other side of the room, Sorcha then addressed Tyra. "About what we just discussed earlier, I ken you are busy, cousin, but you will be helping me immensely. What with the bairn coming, I dinnae have time to keep an eye on Lachlan, and he has a special place in my heart."

Tyra remained silent, trying to think of a way to get out of the task, when Sorcha continued. "Lachlan has been my loyal guardsman for many years. He has sacrificed much to keep me safe and remain on Henderson land. It must be difficult for a man to be away from home so long. It would mean the world to me and—"

"All right, Sorcha, stop your blathering. I will do it, but I will not like it!" Tyra replied.

"Thank you, Tyra. I ken you will make Lachlan a very happy man," Sorcha said. She was beaming with joy.

Tyra frowned in confusion.

"With your planning, I mean," Sorcha said to cover her slip.

Tyra sighed and said, "If you will excuse me, I must return to the glen."

Sorcha nodded.

After Tyra left, the MacGregor women eagerly took their seats at the table, and Amelia said, "Talk now, Sorcha. What are you playing at?"

"Aye, and why do Lachlan and Tyra look as if they want to tear each other's garments off?" Zala asked.

"If we were not here, I do believe they would've started rutting on the floor," Clarissa said.

"Ris! How vulgar you've become. The term is 'making love'. There is no rutting talk here. I fear you've been hanging about with your pirates too long," Amelia chided.

"They're not pirates. They're smugglers, Amie, there is a difference," Clarissa said, rolling her eyes. Clarissa had a long history of working with French smugglers at a cove in England.

Zala just chuckled, and Sorcha grinned, then said, "Sisters, I must tell you about my plan to force Tyra and Lachlan together."

"Is this plan likely to go awry?" Clarissa asked.

"Most certainly," Sorcha replied.

"Then start talking," Zala said and rubbed her hands with glee.

Sorcha went about explaining her method. She told them about her ruse to pretend to find a woman for Lachlan from the village and her insistence that Tyra help Lachlan plan his wedding in his bride's absence.

"Tis very clever. It will mean they will have to spend much time in each other's company," Amelia said.

"But what if they end up killing each other instead?" Clarissa asked.

"Tis not possible. I ken Lachlan is smitten with Tyra. He is just a stubborn goat and has been for years," Zala replied.

Sorcha added, "And Tyra has strong feelings for him too. I sensed it before she and Bram captured me in Glenorchy. Tyra had that look of a woman in love. Twas a pity things took a strange turn. But if they spend more time together, I'm sure they'll see how perfect they are for one another."

Chapter 4

Respect

Lachlan was livid. He stormed out of the solar and down towards the hall. He did not want a wife at all or Sorcha interfering with his life. But there was no way he was going to watch warriors flirt with Tyra right in front of him without feeling some jealousy. He agreed to Sorcha's plans so he could rub it in Tyra's face that he had moved on. If only the attraction he still felt for Tyra would abate. He was like a wild beast in a constant state of arousal and rage. He wanted Tyra so badly, but he could not reconcile that she had pretended to love him when his heart had been fully engaged. He could not trust himself or his feelings.

"Lachlan, slow down. I need a word with you," Bram said as he came up behind him. They continued walking towards the hall.

"If it's about my supposed marriage, you needn't bother. I'll do what needs done."

"Aye, tis partly that, but tis also more."

"What else is there?"

"You ken Tyra is my cousin, and I'm protective of her like she is my sister?"

"Aye, and what of it?"

"My wife has a good heart, and she means to make everyone happy around her. Sometimes she might overstep, but tis with good intentions."

"Will you be getting to the point anytime soon, Laird?" Lachlan asked impatiently.

"Och, calm down. All right then. Tis clear to me there is no love lost between you and Tyra. And I ken you still have anger towards her."

"Aye, I do."

"Lachlan, that anger is misdirected. Twas I who put Tyra in that position, and she did her duty for the good of Clan Henderson."

Lachlan snorted and shook his head.

Bram said, "I'm telling you now, you'll not find a woman with more integrity than Tyra. Once her loyalty is given, she will never betray you, and she is a solid force by your side when things get hard. Lord kens, I leaned on her support in the past when the previous laird tried to crush us."

"Why are you telling me this?"

"Because she deserves your respect, not your ire."

Lachlan remained silent.

Bram sighed. "All I ask is that you allow Tyra to help you because Sorcha will insist upon it. Try not to give her too much grief. Tyra has borne your anger long enough."

Lachlan simply nodded.

Stranger Things

WHEN BRAM AND LACHLAN entered the hall, they noticed the Henderson and MacGregor men were seated together in discussion.

Niall approached them.

Bram asked, "What is it? The women said you were looking for me?"

"There's a small matter of concern. I think it best I address the group."

When they were seated around the table, Niall asked, "Have any of you seen Yesenda MacDonald today?"

Everyone shook their heads.

Lachlan decided to answer, but he selected his words carefully. "Aye, I saw her this morn in the passageway outside my chamber. Why?"

"Did you notice anything strange about her?" Niall asked.

"Not really, although I sensed she was trying to avoid someone," Lachlan replied. He breathed a sigh of relief when no one asked him any further questions.

But it was short-lived when Iain asked, "What was she doing outside your chambers? There's no reason for her to be on that side of the Keep."

"All I ken is she was there, and she left in a hurry." Lachlan knew that was the best explanation he could give and the one which was primarily truthful by omission.

Iain gave him a skeptical look.

"What has happened?" Bram asked.

"There's a stranger in the village; he will not give his name, but he has been asking about her. He did not mention her specifically, but he described her likeness. He said she was recently from an abbey, and he was hoping to see her."

"Why is this of concern?" Beiste asked.

Bram replied, "Her brother Ruadh asked me to keep an eye on her while she is here. He mentioned that sometimes trouble follows Yesenda about."

"What kind of trouble?" Dalziel asked.

"Ruadh did not elaborate; he just said she gets herself involved in minor skirmishes and finds herself in dangerous situations."

"I dinnae want any of that trouble to harm my kin while we're here," Beiste said.

Niall agreed. "I have placed a watcher on the stranger to ensure we ken his whereabouts at all times."

"I will tell my men to remain vigilant. Ensure the women and bairns are closely guarded until we take our leave," Brodie said.

"It would also be in your best interest, Bram, to have someone keep a close eye on Yesenda at all times," Dalziel added.

"I'll do it," Iain volunteered without hesitation.

They all agreed.

It was at that moment the subject of their discussion strolled into the hall. She smiled at several people.

Bram called her over to the group. "Yesenda, a stranger is asking about you in the village. Do you ken who he might be or why?"

She had a surprised expression when she said, "I do not ken. What does this person look like?"

Lachlan observed her and knew she was hiding something, but he kept silent.

Niall replied, "Male, medium height with fair hair. Blue eyes, and he dressed like a pilgrim. He had markings on his forearm."

"What kind?" she asked.

"Twas a spiked war club."

Yesenda frowned, then schooled her features. "I am at a loss. I ken nothing."

Bram said, "I will make more inquiries. In the meantime, you are to remain close to the Keep. Iain will accompany you if you need to go beyond the gates."

Yesenda started to protest, "Laird, tis not necessary, really. I am certain Iain has far more pressing concerns to—"

"You'll not leave this Keep without me, and that's final," Iain growled.

Yesenda glanced at the men and could see none would relent, so she took the path of least resistance and agreed. "Of course, I thank ye, Laird, and Iain; I will be sure to notify you if I leave the Keep."

Iain nodded and gestured for her to take a seat beside him for the noonday meal. Yesenda complied. When the food was served, she closed her eyes and quietly murmured something before she ate.

"What were you doing?" Iain asked.

"Giving thanks," she replied.

"For your food?"

"Aye. There were times in the abbey when we had to give our share to the poor. Food was scarce, so I've learned to give thanks when I have it," she said as she took a massive bite of the pie. "Oh my, this is the best pie I have ever tasted," she groaned as she chewed, utterly oblivious to the effect her words had on the listener.

Iain observed the way Yesenda savored the pie, then for the first time in a long time, he smiled, and this time it reached his eyes.

Stalker

LATER THAT DAY, TYRA made her way back to the glen. It was not far from the Keep. As she walked through the wooded pathway, she felt that she was being watched. She picked up her pace and scanned her surroundings. She knew she was safe on Henderson land. There were guardsmen around, but still, it was an eerie feeling.

Tyra kept her hand on her dirk while carrying her basket in the other. She heard a footstep and ducked behind a tree, crouching down as she kept her eyes peeled towards the woods. Her heart was racing as she tried to listen for any unusual noise. But there was no sound.

She heard soft steps and remained completely still. Another rustling sound could be heard as someone approached. She took a deep breath then jumped out from behind the tree, yelling at the stalker.

Tyra heard a woman shout in fright, and before she knew it, she was relieved of her dirk and thrown into the air, landing on her back, winded.

She blinked up at the sky, trying to catch her breath when Yesenda appeared above her.

"Tyra! I'm so sorry. What the devil were you thinking jumping out of the bushes with a dirk? I could've killed you!" Yesenda reprimanded. She crouched down and helped get Tyra onto her feet.

"Someone was following me; I didnae ken twas you." Tyra coughed as she tried to catch her breath. Yesenda tapped her on the back.

"Where did you learn that move? You disarmed me so fast," Tyra asked.

"I will teach you someday. But who do you think was following you?"

"I dinnae ken, but I had a strange feeling of being watched."

Yesenda quickly scanned the area. She returned Tyra's dirk and said, "We best keep moving. Tis not good to dally in the open."

They made their way to the longhouse.

"Yesenda, were you headed somewhere when I interrupted you?" Tyra asked.

"I just felt like a walk. I dinnae like being in a Keep; there are too many people. I am used to silence, and Keeps are noisy, especially all the creaking floorboards at night."

"You are welcome to stay in Willa's old cottage near mine. Tis quiet in the glen. Iain and I prefer it."

"Iain? Damn, I forgot."

"Forgot what?"

"I was not to leave the Keep without his escort. I didnae intend to walk so far."

"I'm sure Iain will not mind. Besides, if you remain in the glen, he'll eventually see you when he returns home."

When they arrived at the longhouse, there was a line of patients waiting outside for Tyra.

"Do you need help?" Yesenda asked.

"If you have spare time, I dinnae mind. I can always use extra hands."

"I prefer to be useful. I dinnae like to be idle." Yesenda followed Tyra into the longhouse, and they spent the next two hours treating the crofters and villagers. They were so engrossed in their work they did not notice the arrival of the others until a shadow crossed over Tyra as she mixed a poultice.

Lachlan filled the doorway and walked in. His eyes glanced past Tyra, and then he looked to Yesenda.

"She's here," he called out to someone outside.

Moments later, Iain's large frame filled the doorway. "What did I tell you about not leaving the Keep without me?" Iain growled at Yesenda.

"I am sorry; I saw Tyra and decided to help here. I didnae mean to—"

Before Yesenda could finish her sentence, Iain strode right towards her and clasped her hand in his. He then turned and began pulling her towards the door.

"What are you doing?" she protested.

"Taking you back to the Keep."

"But Tyra needs my help."

"Amelia will be here shortly; you're not needed."

"Iain, stop! I told Yesenda she can stay in Willa's cottage," Tyra said.

Iain paused. "She canna stay there. 'Tis already occupied."

"Who's there?" Tyra asked in confusion.

Iain did not say anything. He just clenched his jaw and tried to communicate something with his eyes. Then Tyra got mad when she realized who he meant.

"Iain Henderson, you get Liosa out of there!" Tyra ranted. Her hands were firmly on her hips.

Lachlan and Yesenda looked on in confusion at the silent stare-off between siblings. Iain still clutched Yesenda's hand, and Tyra glowered at him.

Exasperated, Iain replied, "She has nowhere else to go, Tyra. There are things you dinnae ken, and I will not discuss it here. Liosa needs to remain until I can make other arrangements."

"Hello? Tis just me. Is it all right to come in?" Amelia asked as she interrupted their discussion. She hovered just outside the door. Kieran was standing behind her, holding a basket full of healing remedies.

"Aye, of course, please come in. Iain and Lachlan were just leaving," Tyra said as she brushed past Lachlan and ushered Amelia and Kieran inside.

Amelia asked, "Will you be joining us today, Yesenda?"

"Aye," Yesenda replied.

"No," Iain said at the same time.

There was silence again and a weird tension in the room. It was broken by the arrival of yet another person.

Liosa stepped inside the longhouse. "Iain? I thought I heard you. You promised to take me to the markets today."

Now everyone was watching the exchange between Iain and Liosa.

"It will need to wait. I have to escort someone back to the Keep," he replied.

Liosa glanced at Iain clutching Yesenda's hand, and a flash of anger marred her expression, but she rallied. "Then I shall come with you. I miss seeing my old friends at the Keep."

"Liosa, now is not a good time. As you can see, Iain has his hands full," Tyra said.

"Tyra," Iain said in a warning tone.

Sensing the tension in the room, Amelia waded in, taking on the mantle of a consummate peacemaker and matriarch. "Iain, take this lovely lass who I dinnae ken, to the village. Yesenda, you're staying with me. I need extra hands. Kieran, you can leave the basket on the table then please yourself. When I am finished here, we will welcome your escort back to the Keep."

Kieran nodded and left the basket, then moved outdoors.

"Tis a sound plan. Iain, let's go before the market stalls close," Liosa said before she physically separated Iain's hand from Yesenda's. She then pulled him towards the door.

Iain paused and addressed Yesenda. "Dinnae leave this cottage until I return for you."

Yesenda just nodded. Liosa tugged Iain's hand, and they left.

"And what about me, Mistress?" Lachlan asked.

Amelia replied, "You can sit by Tyra and discuss your wedding plans before your bride arrives."

Lachlan grimaced at the prospect then sat down beside Tyra. "Very well, if I must," he said.

Tyra bit her tongue to prevent a derogatory response. She put her head down and continued with her task, ignoring Lachlan completely.

Despite his outward show of disinterest, Lachlan struggled to keep his eyes off her.

Chapter 5

Whiskey

After the women completed their task, Lachlan and Kieran escorted Amelia back to the Keep while Yesenda remained behind with Tyra. It was late afternoon, and they were preparing vegetables for supper when Fia, Bram's mother, and Willa, Bram's sister, appeared at the door. They looked livid.

"I need a dram of your whiskey," Fia said as she strode straight towards the table.

"So do I," Willa said as she followed behind.

"What is it? What has happened?" Tyra asked. She stood, grabbed the whiskey bottle off the mantle, and filled two cups for Fia and Willa to drink.

Fia plonked herself on one of the chairs, and when the cup was placed in front of her, she drank the whole lot in one go. She slammed it on the table and said, "Another, please."

Tyra obliged.

Fia threw back that cup as well. "Keep them coming, Tyra. I dinnae ken why you keep such dainty wee cups. Do you not have bigger ones?" she asked as she looked around the room.

"Would you prefer a bucket, Aunty?" Tyra smirked.

"If you have one handy, I'll not refuse."

"All right, what is it, Aunt Fia? Is it the bairns? Bram? Niall?"

Willa emptied her cup and said, "'Tis far worse."

"Tell me."

"Tis your brother, Iain, and that wretched woman, Liosa!"

"What has happened now?" Tyra took a seat.

"We were at the markets today, and Liosa came marching into the village, flouncing about like she is the queen of Alba," Fia snorted in disgust.

"Then she flirted with every vendor and village male while showing off Iain's ring on her finger like she's spoken for," Willa said.

Tyra just shook her head. "Iain has nothing but air between his ears when it comes to her. She is currently using your old cottage, Willa."

Willa slammed the cup on the table. "I should hope not!"

"Tis true. I wanted Yesenda to stay there, but Iain said tis occupied."

Yesenda sat quietly, shelling beans for the pottage when she asked, "Who is she?"

"Trouble and woe. That's who," Fia replied.

Tyra said, "We all grew up together. Liosa's family worked the croft not far from Da's holding. Iain was smitten the moment he first clapped eyes on her, but Liosa set her cap on Bram early on."

"Aye, that she did, and I threatened to kill her in her sleep if she tried anything with my brother," Willa said.

"When she could not get her claws into Bram, she latched onto Iain, encouraging him to challenge Cruim for the lairdship, and of course, he did what she suggested," Tyra said. She picked up a large knife and started cutting some cabbage.

"So, what happened?" Yesenda asked.

"Iain was half beaten to death for the slight. Bram saved his life, and Tyra and Ma had to nurse him back to health," Willa replied.

"And what of Liosa?" Yesenda asked.

"That trollop did not even stick around to see if he survived. She berated him for losing the challenge then scurried off to who kens where," Willa replied.

"Why is she here now?" Yesenda asked.

"Liosa comes and goes as she pleases. They are together, then she causes trouble, and they part ways. She returns if she hears word that Iain might be losing interest," Tyra replied.

Willa just nodded and poured herself another cup.

"Like the time Iain courted a bonnie lass from Glasgow. Liosa got wind of it and reappeared long enough to assert her claim, then she was gone again. Tis the same pattern over and over," Fia said as she shelled peas.

"We dinnae like her for Iain. He deserves far better," Willa grumbled.

"Where does she go after they part ways?" Yesenda asked.

"That's the troubling thing. We dinnae ken, but we believe there is a wealthy merchant somewhere. One does not wear her fine garments without a steady supply of coin. Iain has begged for her hand in marriage many times, but she refuses," Tyra replied.

"And yet she will not let him go. She does not want him, but she cannot bear for him to find someone else," Yesenda said.

"Aye. It will take a miracle before Iain realizes she is not worth it," Willa replied.

"People change sometimes. Mayhap one day, she will accept his proposal," Yesenda said.

"Bite your tongue, Yesenda MacDonald! That will be the day they imprison me for her murder," Fia said, scowling at her.

"Sorry, Fia, I didnae mean any harm by it."

"Well, we can only hope that her stay this time is short," Tyra said.

"If not, I am prepared to kick her bahookie out of my cottage and hurl her off a cliff," Willa said.

Yesenda grinned.

"Cousin, such violence. Living in the woods has turned you into a slaugh."

Willa chuckled at Tyra's comment.

"I fear Willa has turned into a baobhan sith. She resembled a feral vampire when she emerged from the woods," Fia said with a smirk.

The women started laughing. Soon they were all preparing vegetables and partaking of the whiskey.

Willa asked, "And what of you, Tyra? How are things with Lachlan?"

Tyra blushed. "There is nothing between Lachlan and me, nothing at all. Why? Have you heard something?"

"Calm down. I meant, how go the wedding plans? Sorcha told me she has charged you with planning his wedding."

"Oh... that. Lachlan told me he does not care. He is happy to do whatever his bride wants."

"Aye, most men only care about wine and rutting through the wedding night," Fia replied.

"Ma! Dinnae be so vulgar. We have a guest," Willa said.

"Och, she's a MacDonald. I'm sure she has heard what men are like," Fia replied.

"But she is practically a nun," Willa whispered to her mother.

Yesenda burst out laughing. "'Tis all right, Willa, I am not offended. I may have been raised in an abbey, but I can assure you, I am not a nun."

The Wager

LACHLAN ENTERED THE Village Inn. His hair was partially wet, having bathed in the river earlier. He wore a new change of garments, favoring his white leine, and he was ready to join Kieran and drink himself into oblivion. It had been a taxing day; spending several hours sitting beside Tyra was torture. Her alluring scent permeated his senses, and he had to clench his fists several times to stop from reaching out and tucking a loose tendril of hair behind her ear. Lachlan could not ignore those dimples and those eyes when she turned to ask him questions about his blasted wedding. They pierced his soul. She was breaking down his resistance, and she did not even know it.

Lachlan made his way to the trestle tables down the back of the inn, where Kieran sat near other warriors. Food and ale were already being served.

"So, who are you trying to impress?" Kieran asked.

"No one," Lachlan replied as he took a seat on the bench.

"But you smell nice, and you're wearing your fine garments. Has a wench taken your fancy?"

"I dinnae care about wenches. I just want to fill my belly and drink some ale."

"Hmm, spoken like a man with woman problems," Kieran replied as he chewed on roasted venison.

"Haud yer wheesht, Kieran. Eat your food," Lachlan grumbled.

A comely serving woman approached their table. She gave Lachlan a come-hither look and said, "You're a braw one. We dinnae see the likes of you around here oft. Is there anything I can get you? Food? Ale? A companion for the night?"

"Food and ale will do," Lachlan replied, making it clear he wanted nothing more.

The woman sighed, "Verra well, the braw ones are always taken."

Thirty minutes later, they had finished their meal and were onto their third jug of ale. Lachlan felt that pleasant tingling feeling of being slightly tipsy but not too drunk when loud, raucous laughter could be heard from the opposite table. One voice in particular grated on Lachlan's nerves. It was Dermid, the warrior he had seen Tyra with earlier. Lachlan watched him and clenched his jaw. He had to admit, Dermid was a handsome man, and he could see why the women in the Keep blushed whenever he winked at them.

Lachlan took another large swig of his ale and listened in to their conversation.

"I'm telling you, lads, she's mine. She finds me funny, and she has really taken a shine to me. Which means I have a chance."

"Och-ho, you wish, Dermid. She is most likely laughing at you and not your jokes!" A guardsman, Connor, piped in. That had all the men chuckling.

"Who are they talking about?" Lachlan asked Kieran.

"I dinnae ken; they're just fools blathering on about how big their cocks are," Kieran replied.

Lachlan listened some more.

"Mark my words, within the sennight, I'll have her eating out of the palm of my hands," Dermid said.

"If she kenned where your hands have been, she'd keep her mouth away," Connor said. That had the decibels rising as the other men roared with laughter.

Dermid stood and issued a challenge, "Are you willing to wager on it? I bet you a day's coin that within the next two days, I'll have her bedded, and in a fortnight, she'll be wed to me."

Connor stopped laughing and warned, "Careful, lad. Dinnae speak out of turn. She's still the laird's cousin."

Lachlan's head whipped to the side when he realized Dermid was talking about Tyra. He glared at Dermid and saw red.

And that's when all hell broke loose.

"Lach, no!" Kieran yelled, but it was too late.

Lachlan was over the table and on the other side of the room, one hand clutching Dermid's collar while his other hand was curled into a fist as he repeatedly punched Dermid in the face. Dermid swiped Lachlan's legs, and they hit the floor, still punching, kicking, and rolling on the ground.

Connor and Kieran were in there trying to separate them, but Lachlan would not stop.

"You're a scunner! I bet you a day's wages she'll be mine before you can even get your filthy paws on her!" Lachlan shouted at Dermid.

"You better have the sceats because I already ken you will lose," Dermid yelled in reply before they were finally on their feet and separated.

Connor held onto Dermid, and Kieran had Lachlan.

Clarity

THE FOLLOWING DAY, Lachlan woke to someone kicking his foot. He opened his eyes and groaned when he saw Kieran glaring down at him.

"You daft prick," Kieran said.

Lachlan squinted to block out the sunlight. "What do you want?" he grumbled. Every bone in his body ached from the night before, and his head pounded from too much ale. "What are you doing in my room? Dinnae tell me Yesenda is here as well."

"Why would Yesenda be in your room?"

Lachlan quickly sobered and shook his head. It was fuzzy, and he needed to shut his mouth.

"Nothing, what do you want, Kieran?"

"You drunken lout. You dinnae remember what you did last night, do you?"

Lachlan sat up; the room spun slightly, but he rubbed his face. His hair was disheveled, and he was shirtless.

"What about last night?"

"You set a wager with that stupid pup Dermid that you could bed Tyra first."

"I did no such thing! I was defending her honor."

"Be that as it may. It appears the wager is in play, and guess where Dermid is headed right now?"

Lachlan frowned and asked, "Where?"

Kieran replied, "To the longhouse to get his cuts attended to by *your* woman."

Lachlan was off the bed in an instant. His head spun, and he stumbled slightly, then righted himself. "That whoreson bastard. He needs to stay away from her. Someone needs to warn Tyra about him."

Lachlan was trying to put a shirt on and reach for his sword when Kieran said, "Lach, you look like shite, and you reek of stale ale and horse piss. If you wanna woo your woman, I suggest you take a bath first."

Lachlan paused, looking down at the state of himself. He sniffed his armpit and grimaced then said, "Aye, you're right."

Kieran just shook his head as Lachlan half rushed, mostly stumbled about the room in a panic.

With a single-minded purpose to win Tyra, Lachlan grabbed his things and made his way to the river for a thorough washing. He was determined to win at all costs. Gone was the anger he held against Tyra, all of it gone. He saw everything with vivid clarity. The thought of her with anyone else was something he could not bear.

He was just about out of the Keep when he heard Sorcha calling him. She seemed concerned about something.

He paused. "Are you all right, Sorcha? Is it the bairn? Are you hale?" he asked impatiently.

"I'm fine, but it's about your bride from the village," she replied.

"There's no need, Sorcha. I dinnae want a bride from the village. I have to go." Lachlan tried to shuffle past her, but she blocked his way.

"No, I *really* need to tell you something about her, Lach—"

"I dinnae have the time, Sorcha; can you tell me about it later? I have something of great importance to attend to." He moved around her.

"But she's—"

"Whatever it is, I'll see to it later," he yelled over his shoulder as he started running.

Chapter 6

Smooth

"Ouch! It stings," Dermid said as Tyra applied a salve to his cuts.

He was sitting on her tall bench in the longhouse, shirtless and casually dangling his legs over the side, just gazing at her as she used a soft cloth to dab the ointment under his ribcage.

"Lift your arm," she said.

He did as requested, and Tyra worked on the abrasions across his ribs. She ducked under his arm and moved to his front.

"Your ribs are bruised. Whoever hit you had perfect aim."

"Och, you should see the state he's in. He is most likely dead now," Dermid joked.

Tyra grinned. "Does it hurt when I press here?" she asked as she applied pressure with her palm to his rib.

"No, but it does hurt somewhere else."

She raised her brow and asked, "Where?"

Dermid took her hand and placed it over his heart. "It hurts right here, my heart. It aches for you, Tyra," he whispered.

Tyra pulled her hand away and rolled her eyes. "Dinnae play games, Dermid. 'Tis serious."

Dermid reached out to draw her nearer, so she was standing between his thighs; one arm was looped around her back. "I am serious, Tyra. Whenever I see you, I ache... in two places."

"I dinnae want to ken the other place," she replied.

Changing tack, he said, "Well, in all seriousness, I do ache in the other places as well, which is why I came to see you."

Tyra was skeptical. She tried to move out of his grasp, but he held her firm.

"Dermid, you need to let me go and cease this silliness."

"What if I dinnae want to let you go?" He caressed her cheek with the back of his hand. "You're a bonnie woman, Tyra." Dermid tentatively leaned forward and whispered in her ear, "You're the kind of lass a man marries and makes bairns with." He kissed the area below her ear and pulled her even closer as he followed a trail of kisses lower.

Maybe it was because she had felt so rejected lately by Lachlan, or because Dermid was easy on the eyes; Tyra was not sure why, but she did not push him away. It felt good being with a man who was not always angry with her. A man who desired her.

Tyra closed her eyes as Dermid pulled her even closer, and his hands began to roam. Tyra let him, but she felt torn between the need to be wanted and the sense that his touch felt wrong to her somehow.

Dermid whispered, "Come home with me, Tyra. I want you in my bed."

She opened her eyes at the word 'bed' and realized she did not want that with Dermid or just any man. She quickly nudged him away.

"I'm sorry, Dermid, but I canna do that." She quickly changed the subject. "I dinnae need to apply a bandage to your ribs. They are tender, but time will rid them of the bruising. If that is all for today, then I think 'tis best you go," she said, taking on her role as a healer again.

Dermid was silent, contemplating something. Then he said, "I desire you, Tyra, I always have, but I will not press my suit... until you are ready to welcome it."

"I will not welcome it, Dermid, so unless there's something else that ails you, I have much to do."

Taking a different approach, Dermid replied, "There is one more thing. I think my attacker might have kicked me in the pecker. My bawsack is really bruised, and I'm afraid nothing down there will work again. Could you see to just make sure it's hale?"

Tyra gave him a skeptical look.

"I am in earnest. I am hoping my cock is not broken because I need my bollocks to sire bairns."

Tyra folded her arms and kept staring at him, and Dermid did not flinch. His face remained stoic.

She sighed. "All right, I'll have a look."

Dermid slowly lowered his trews and lay back on the bench. "'Tis just the groin area really that needs some attention."

Tyra went straight into healer mode. Amelia had taught her how to administer to that area. She placed a cloth over it, providing a barrier for her hand, and then she applied pressure around the underside of his groin as she tried to feel for any lumps.

"Aye, right there, Tyra, that exact spot. Och, I feel it getting better already, lass."

Tyra looked closely for any lesions. As soon as she touched his member, it swelled in her cloth-covered hand and rose to attention. "Och, Tyra, you've healed me; it works just fine!"

"Bloody guttersnipe! You tricked me." Tyra scowled as Dermid burst out laughing.

At that moment, the door flew open, and Lachlan stood on the threshold. He glared at the sight before him. He roared, "Get away from her!" and then he lost his ever-loving mind.

"Lachlan!" Tyra screamed as he launched himself at Dermid.

Dermid tumbled off the bench and rolled head over naked arse onto the floor as Lachlan followed with fists flying.

Wreck and Ruin

"I AM SORRY, TYRA."

"Are you? Are you sorry? Look at what you've done to my cottage, Lachlan!" Tyra yelled.

Lachlan was standing in the middle of the longhouse surveying the carnage he had wrought fifteen minutes earlier. The bench was broken. Several pots and jars lay smashed on the floor, their contents oozing on the ground. A partly broken chair was hanging from a rafter.

"I will clean it," Lachlan said.

Tyra just shook her head. She was standing by the table mixing a salve for his cuts.

"And look at the sorry state of you. Your eye is swollen, you're bleeding all over my floor, and you broke Dermid's pecker!" she shouted the last five words.

Dermid was passed out on the table with a cold compress on his head and his groin.

Lachlan chortled, then stopped when Tyra gave him a death stare.

"What were you thinking tearing in here like Black Donald himself? I had just treated Dermid's cuts."

"It didnae look like his cuts you were treating," Lachlan snorted.

Tyra stormed over to him. She was livid now. She stood on tiptoes and got right in his face, pointing her finger at him. "You dinnae have the right to enter my cottage and attack my patrons!"

"You had your hand on his cock!" Lachlan growled.

"I'm a healer. I was treating an injury."

Lachlan scoffed, "From what I saw, there was nothing wrong with that part of him."

"You are the most stubborn man I have ever had the misfortune to meet. 'Tis not your concern what I do with my patrons in my own cottage. You dinnae attack anyone while I am treating them," she yelled.

Lachlan watched Tyra rant and scold him, and for some reason, it just turned him on. She was a spitfire when mad, and Lachlan wanted to haul her over his shoulder, throw her on the bed, and silence her with passion. He smiled at the thought.

"What are you smirking at? You think this is funny?" She whacked his arm.

"Ouch, no, love," he said, immediately wiping the grin from his face.

Tyra just shook her head again. "Find a chair you have not broken and sit down. I'll see to your cuts as well." Lachlan did as told. Tyra returned and applied a salve to Lachlan's eye, then she saw to his knuckles. She was fuming the whole time.

Lachlan just gazed at her and memorized every aspect of her loveliness.

"You're going to help me clean up this mess, then return Dermid to the Keep when I've tended to him."

"Aye," Lachlan replied, and he reached across and pulled a loose tendril back, tucking it behind her ear.

Tyra ignored the pleasant sensation and refused to make eye contact with Lachlan again.

"Tyra."

"What?" she snapped.

"From now on, I will be present if you need to treat a man's pecker."

"What are you on about now?" She looked up in confusion.

"You heard me. You will not touch any other man's nether regions unless I am here with you to make sure he does not take any liberties."

"You're daft. I will do whatever I please, and you have no say in it." She tied off the bandage and ignored him.

"Tyra, look at me," Lachlan growled.

She gave him her eyes.

"Tonight, we are going to have a talk about the future."

"I dinnae want to talk about anything with you," she huffed.

"'Tis about my wedding, Tyra, and I need you to tell me what you think my bride would like on her wedding day. Sorcha said you have to help me." His gaze bore into hers.

"Fine," she snapped. "We can talk tonight."

"In the hall."

"Very well, in the hall."

"I'll hold you to it, lass."

At that moment, Dermid groaned as he was coming around. Tyra moved to tend to him.

Lachlan grabbed her arm and pulled her back towards him. "I mean it, if you're not in the hall tonight, I will find you."

Tyra thought about Lachlan's wedding, and her heart sank again. She had forgotten that the most infuriating man on the planet still had an effect on her. For the first time ever, Tyra envied his bride.

Best Laid Plans

"AMIE! YOU HAVE TO HELP me. I have made a muckle of a mess."

The MacGregor women were in Sorcha's private chambers, and she was pacing the floor.

"Why? What have you done, Sorcha?"

"You ken the plan I had to force Tyra and Lachlan together?"

"Aye," Amelia replied.

"Part of the plan was to pretend Lachlan was courting a woman in the village. I heard there was a lady from the village. She has recently arrived; I've never met her before. I did not even find out her name. Bram's men said she was bonnie; the women said she was friendly—"

"Sorcha, will you be getting to the point anytime soon?" Zala asked.

"Right, well I thought there'd be no harm in getting them to invite her to the Keep just to add to the ruse."

"Well, that sounds harmless," Clarissa replied.

"It is anything but... it's so terrible, I canna believe it."

Amelia asked, "So, what happened?"

"It turns out, the woman I chose just happens to be..."

"Happens to be?" Clarissa asked.

"Heather O'Connell!" Sorcha shouted.

Zala sat up straighter and shook her head. "No, tell me it's not her?"

"Who's she?" Clarissa asked.

"It's Heather? The Heather?" Zala asked.

Sorcha nodded and looked as if she was on the verge of tears.

"Damn!" Zala said and started pacing the room alongside Sorcha.

"Who the bloody hell is Heather O'Connell?" Amelia raised her voice in exasperation.

"Heather is Lachlan's first love. The one who ran away with his best friend on the eve of their wedding day. He was heartbroken. Walked around moping about Glenorchy until Brodie made him a guardsman," Zala replied.

"Good Lord," Amelia said.

"What are the odds? You have the worst luck, Sorcha!" Clarissa said in disbelief.

"Aye, Sorcha, you do beat all," Zala added.

"'Tis easily fixed. You can just uninvite her," Amelia said.

"That's the problem, Amie. She's already here, and she is excited to meet Lachlan. What if he falls for her again?" Sorcha asked.

Amelia replied, "Dinnae fash. It does not matter. Heather is a married woman, and Lachlan would never court a married woman even if he still had feelings for her."

"She's widowed now," Sorcha said.

"Oh shit," Amelia replied.

"I tried to warn Lachlan this morn, but he was in a hurry. He has no idea she is here, and now he will never be with Tyra, and I have ruined both of their lives!" With those words, Sorcha burst into tears.

Amelia was instantly by her side. "Sister, calm down. 'Tis not good for the bairn."

"I ken it," Sorcha sniffed. "I canna help it. I keep crying, and I feel so bad. 'Tis my fault for bringing that unfaithful wench here," she said while sobbing.

"You are overwrought with emotion, 'tis all. Sometimes bairns can do that." Amelia hugged her and soothed her gently. She glanced at Zala and Clarissa and mouthed, "Say something!"

Zala said, "Sorcha, dinnae fash yourself, I will make sure Lachlan ends up with Tyra even if I have to throw Heather into a bog pit."

"Or push her into the freezing river," Clarissa added.

That had Sorcha giggling through sniffles.

"All will be well, Sorcha. Lachlan was heartbroken when Heather left him, but it was years ago now, and I'm sure if he saw her again, anger, not love, would be the only feeling," Zala said in a gentle voice.

Sorcha nodded her head. "That gives me some hope. I am so blessed to have you all here with me."

"That's what sisters are for. Everything will turn out well in the end," Amelia replied with a determined look on her face.

The Pilgrim

SEVERAL MILES AWAY, in an inn at Glencoe Village, a weary pilgrim stood bare-chested by the fireplace. He had scars along his back, remnants of a severe whipping. On his forearm, he bore a tattoo: a spike-head war club crossed over a mace. It was an emblem of a religious order. He wore a drying cloth around his waist, having just bathed. As he drank his whiskey, he stared into the leaping flames of the fire.

"Will you be standing there all night? I'm sure you'll find more pleasure over here."

Thoughts of his mission foremost on his mind, he had almost forgotten about the sultry wench currently naked and spread-eagle on his bed.

He placed the empty cup on the mantle, then slowly strode toward the bed. He gazed down at the buxom woman who lay there, her thighs splayed wide open for him. The reddish hue of her woman's heart was unmissable. Her pleasure button protruded from her nether lips and glistened with her arousal. He gazed at her hardened nipples and succulent breasts as he licked his lips and released the towel.

She gasped at the sight of him. Curiosity and arousal combined as she studied his erect manhood. Its tip was pierced with a silver ball, and two more silver bars pierced through the sides.

He stroked himself to full length as he gazed at her. "It has been a long time, my darling. I trust there has been no one else since me."

"Aye, my love, only you."

"If you are lying, I will ken it," he said.

He leaned over and captured a nipple in his mouth as he tongued the flesh. Her breathing became erratic. Then he moved his hand between her thighs and applied pressure against her button with his thumb.

She moaned and threw her head back.

"You are ready for me so soon?"

"Aye, I need you. You have been away too long."

"Have you taken the herb? I do not want my seed to take root."

She nodded.

"Good," he replied as he joined her on the bed and settled his hips between her thighs. He placed his length at her entrance, and with both hands, he held her wrists above her head. Then he thrust inside her and groaned with pleasure.

She gasped at the invasion, and the exquisite feeling of his piercings brushing against her inner walls sent her into a flurry. "Aye, that feels so good," she moaned.

Anger flickered across his eyes as he increased his thrusts. Before, he had wanted to make it pleasurable and take his time, but now he just sought release. His strokes became more brutal and rougher as he pounded deep inside. He opened his eyes and watched her breasts bounce with each thrust. He lowered his head and suckled the tips while she shuddered beneath him. Her channel tightened against his length, which confirmed his earlier suspicions.

It was then the pilgrim plundered her body with abandon. She moaned in pleasure, but he had already lost interest. This was no longer enjoyable for him, but his body needed the release because he had been celibate too long, so he forced himself to find it.

She found hers before him, and that triggered his own. When it came, it hit him hard, and he groaned as he released his seed. He thrust several times until he was empty but remained buried deep. His eyes now seared hers.

"My love?" she gasped, still coming down from her orgasm.

He put a hand across her throat and squeezed. "You lied, Liosa, there have been others since me."

Her eyes bulged with fear at the truth of his words. She reached up, trying to pry his hand away as she tried to get air inside her lungs.

He simply watched her struggle. She tried to scratch him and kick him, but he held her firm. Panic flickered with the realization that she was about to die. Her struggle became weaker. Her eyes began to flutter and roll upward with the lack of oxygen.

"Dinnae lie to me again," he growled into her ear. Then he pulled out and released her neck.

The pilgrim got out of the bed and walked over to where her delicate garments lay, garments his liege had bought for her. He heard her coughing and wheezing, trying to force air into her lungs. He did not care. He picked up her clothes and threw them at her.

"Leave before I kill you."

Liosa nodded and flew off the bed, grabbing her things.

The pilgrim retrieved a wet cloth from his bucket and cleaned himself. He threw the material back in the water and strode naked toward the fire again.

He heard the sound of running footsteps as the door closed with Liosa's hasty exit.

"Unfaithful bitch," he muttered.

He poured himself another cup of whiskey and sipped it as he stared back into the flames. His disappointment at Liosa was further proof that women could not be trusted, least of all the woman he sought.

Into the void of an empty room and the sound of the crackling fire, he said, "Miriam Ferguson, I am coming for you."

Chapter 7

The Wooing

That night, the Great Hall was filled with Hendersons and MacGregors, and the atmosphere was festive. It had been a bountiful harvest season. The game was plentiful, and the Henderson clan was thriving. On the main dais sat Beiste and Amelia with Bram, Sorcha, and Yesenda, including their families. The rest sat at trestles spread out across the hall.

Tyra walked into the hall. She had bathed with a few drops of rose water and worn a grey tunic with a matching surcoat. She had embroidered a flowery appliqué design by hand. Her hair was up in a loose bun, so tendrils fell about her neck. She looked radiant, and her natural burnished lips added to the appeal.

Tyra was busy trying to find a spare seat; she failed to see Lachlan leaning casually against the back wall. He had been watching and waiting for her arrival. Before she could walk any further, his arm shot out, and he pulled her gently towards his table. "Over here, love, I saved you a seat."

Tyra had to catch her breath at the sight of Lachlan in his clan plaid, white léine, and coat. His hair was partially wet and combed back, and his rugged jawline made him a striking figure to behold. He was every inch a Highland male, and his eyes bore deep into her soul. He gazed at her, raking his eyes appreciatively over her body. It sent a shiver up her spine.

"You are beautiful, lass. There is nothing bonnier in the Highlands than your rosy dimpled cheeks and sterling eyes."

"Lachlan, dinnae ply me with pretty words; remember you are about to be married."

"Aye, that I am." He held her gaze.

They sat in a quiet corner together as platters of food and drink flowed through the hall. Lachlan served Tyra, placing choice cuts of meat on her plate. He poured her a drink before he set about serving himself. She was embarrassed by his attention but secretly pleased.

When they began eating, Tyra asked, "You wanted to discuss the wedding?"

"Aye, if you were getting married, what would you like to have on your wedding day?"

"I dinnae think it matters what I like, Lachlan. You should think about what your bride favors."

"But I'm asking you. In all honesty, I dinnae ken much about what women prefer, but if you were a bride, what is your greatest wish?"

It was on the tip of Tyra's tongue to say, "My greatest wish would be you." But she refrained.

"Just try to imagine your day, Tyra."

"All right. I would favor a small ceremony in the chapel. I would love my close kin to be there and to marry on Henderson land. I would enjoy a wedding breakfast with simple fare and mayhap a cake and sweet treats for the bairns."

"What of a wedding gift from your husband?" Lachlan asked.

Tyra smiled and replied, "Tis enough for me that he is there and willing to love me for an eternity. If I had his love and he had mine, then I would want for nothing else."

Lachlan paused and just gazed at her. He cleared his throat and said, "What about a keepsake or a trinket?"

"Mayhap a simple band around my finger to bind our vows. But really, Lachlan, you need to ask your bride. She may want something grander."

"No, I ken she is similar to you," he replied.

Tyra asked, "What do you want on your wedding day, as the groom, I mean?"

"I would like Kieran by my side. He is my best friend. I dinnae mind a short chapel service. I'd like ale and food at the wedding and close kin, but really, I dinnae care overly much. As long as my bride is there, and I ken she is mine forever, my heart is more than satisfied. I would also like a gold band on my finger as a symbol of our union to the world."

"Then I think your wedding is arranged, Lachlan. I can talk to Cook to organize the fare, and the blacksmith can forge the bands. You might have to make Kieran presentable, but everything else is easy to arrange."

Lachlan chuckled.

"Speaking of Kieran, where is he tonight? He is usually by your side." No sooner had Tyra asked than Kieran appeared and joined them at the table.

"Och, Tyra, you are a vision. Tis good to see you."

Tyra grinned and replied, "Thank you, Kieran. Have you just finished guard duty?"

"Aye, tis busy in the Keep tonight. There are strangers about and talk of a new lass from the village joining us. I think it has brought out all the unwed men."

Kieran had a fresh trencher of food placed beside him with some cider. A serving woman winked at him then moved on. He ate his fare with gusto. He talked with half a mouthful and asked, "So what have you two been discussing?"

"Tyra has been helping me plan my wedding," Lachlan replied.

"Has she now?" Kieran smirked and kept eating. He turned away from them to talk to others at the table.

"Thank you, Tyra, you've been most helpful," Lachlan said when it was just the two of them again.

They shared a moment and took a large swig of cider. Tyra was warring between enjoying Lachlan's glances and reminding herself he was to be married soon. It was a bittersweet evening, but it seemed as if they had at least made some sort of peace with one another. Lachlan was no longer ignoring her, and she felt as if maybe, over time, her feelings for him would fade into friendship.

That hope was short-lived because no sooner had they settled into a comfortable rapport, Kieran slammed his cup on the table and said, "What the bloody hell is she doing here?"

Tyra felt Lachlan tense immediately, and she sensed eyes on her. She looked up in confusion at the central dais. Sorcha was staring right at her when she paled. Tyra wondered if maybe the babe was upsetting Sorcha. Then she saw the MacGregor women gazing at a point to the right of her. Zala Fletcher was already out of her chair and making her way across the hall.

Tyra turned to her right and saw a woman she had never seen before. She wore delicate garments and seemed nervous. She hovered close to their table.

"Can I help you?" Tyra asked, but the woman did not acknowledge her. Instead, she had her eyes on Lachlan, and she smiled.

Tyra glanced at Lachlan and saw recognition in his eyes, and her heartbeat plummeted. She knew immediately that this was Lachlan's bride.

"Hello, Lachlan."

"Heather."

"May I sit?" she asked.

Tyra felt like an intruder; she tried to stand to offer the woman her seat, but Lachlan's hand clamped down on her thigh as he pulled her back down.

Tyra tried to pry it away, but he locked on like a band of steel.

"I heard you were here. I... I never dreamed I'd see you again." Heather pulled up a seat and moved it opposite them.

"What is this?" Lachlan said.

"What do you mean?" Heather asked.

"What are you doing here?" Lachlan snapped.

"I've come to marry you, Lachlan."

"Over my dead body," Kieran replied.

"Kieran, it has been a long time," Heather said.

"Not long enough," Kieran snorted.

"Well, this is strange. I assumed you wanted to see me, Lachlan. Twas arranged by the laird's wife; she invited me here."

Lachlan glared at the dais and mouthed, "Sorcha!"

Sorcha cringed and quickly ducked her head behind Amelia.

Lachlan murmured to himself, "Trust me to find you a bride, she said. I ken a woman in the village, she said. Tis time you wed, she said."

Zala finally arrived and cut in, "Heather, we are sorry, but there has been some mistake. Come now, I think we need to discuss this in private." Zala practically pulled Heather out of her chair.

They both paused when Lachlan asked, "What of your husband?"

"Davey passed two years ago, tis just me now," Heather replied.

"And you thought you could come in here and marry me?"

"Aye, I have never stopped loving you, Lachlan."

He snorted with disbelief.

Tyra was becoming increasingly uncomfortable. "Lachlan, mayhap you two should go somewhere and talk in private."

"No, the time for talking was years ago," he replied, emphasizing the last part. "Before I stood at the altar and waited for Heather only to find that she'd run off with my best friend."

"I am sorry, Lachlan, truly I am, but I was young and feckless," Heather said.

Zala had called for reinforcements because soon Clarissa was on the other side of Heather and ushering her away.

Lachlan continued to clutch Tyra's hand. He turned to her and said, "She is not my bride-to-be. I have but one woman I wish to spend the rest of my life with. Tyra, there is something I need to ask you and—"

Lachlan's speech was cut short when a panicked Bram shouted, "Tyra!"

Tyra turned her head to the dais and watched the drama unfold. Bram held Sorcha in his arms. Her body was limp. Amelia was issuing orders as the occupants of the dais exited the hall.

Tyra knew that cry. Bram may be a mighty laird, but he was still her cousin, and he needed her.

Into the Thick of It

TYRA SPRINTED OUT OF the hall towards the laird's chamber. She was running up the stairs when she stumbled. Before her head hit the step, strong hands lifted her from behind and placed her back on her feet.

"Careful, love," Lachlan said. He was right behind her.

When they reached the top floor, Tyra noticed Beiste, Brodie, Iain, and Niall were outside.

Beiste said, "They want you inside."

Tyra nodded and entered the chamber while Lachlan remained with the others.

Bram was hovering over Sorcha, clutching her limp hand. When he saw Tyra, he looked relieved.

"All will be well, cousin," Tyra said, and he nodded.

Amelia and Zala were moving about the room like they had done this many times before. Amelia placed her ear over Sorcha's chest, listening to her heart. She positioned Sorcha slightly on her side. Then she felt her stomach.

"What has happened?" Tyra asked.

"Tis most likely she has fainted, but I want to make sure her heart is strong, and the bairn is well."

"Do you feel anything?" Bram asked.

"Aye, the babe moved. But Sorcha's heart is a little slow. She should come around soon."

Zala came over then with strong-smelling salts and placed them under Sorcha's nose.

It was not long before Sorcha opened her eyes.

"Bram? What happened?" Sorcha asked.

Bram and Amelia helped her into a sitting position. Bram kept kissing her cheek and reassuring her.

"You are well, Sorcha. You took on a fainting spell. How do you feel?" Amelia asked.

"I feel fine. I just felt like the world was spinning, and then it all went black."

"Tis time you rested and stopped trying to do too much. Your matchmaking days are over," Zala replied.

Sorcha grinned as relief spread across the room. But within moments, relief turned to concern when Sorcha bent over and grimaced. "Ouch!" she cried and clutched her belly again.

"What is it, love?" Bram asked.

"Aaah!" she groaned and clasped Bram's hand in pain. "Something is happening, Amie, I dinnae feel right."

Amelia glanced at Sorcha's stomach and saw the change to indicate the bairn had shifted lower. She paled.

"What is happening?" Bram asked.

Tyra knew precisely what was happening. She glanced at Amelia and Zala for a moment as she saw the same fear reflected in their eyes. They tried to mask it from Sorcha, but Tyra knew what they knew because they had all witnessed it in the past.

In that moment, the three women were connected, knowing that new life was about to enter the world before its time. Whether mother and child survived the event was a matter for the heavens alone. Yet with that understanding came a silent pact that they would do all in their power to ensure a favorable outcome.

"Bram, Sorcha, tis time to get ready to meet your bairn because this one is impatient to be out in the world," Tyra said.

"No, tis too soon," Sorcha replied, panicked. "It canna survive." She buried her head in Bram's neck, and he just held her tighter. His eyes remained focused on the three women. Fear and concern marred his features.

"Tis true, Sorcha, your bairn is a wee bit early, but not so early that he canna survive," Tyra said.

"Aye, this bairn has MacGregor and Henderson blood in its veins. Two of the most stubborn clans in the Highlands. Dinnae rule them out just yet," Amelia said as she stared at Sorcha, willing her to believe and have faith.

Sorcha nodded with quiet resolve in her tone, "Aye, you're right, Amie, I didnae marry a stubborn ox for nothing!"

"And I didnae marry a fearless wench for nothing!" Bram replied.

"Tis important you remain calm. Ken that you are in good hands," Zala said.

The three women were already on the move. Amelia stepped outside and had a private word with Beiste. He kissed her forehead then squeezed her arm in reassurance. She issued orders to the men for hot water and towels, and various other items from her chamber. Then she requested that they pray because there was only so much human hands could do. Between them, they were going to give it their all.

"Tyra, is there anything you need?" Lachlan asked.

"Aye, Lachie, can you fetch my healer's basket? I keep a spare one in the solar."

Lachlan's eyes softened at her nickname for him. "I'll see to it."

"I am here also if you need me," Yesenda said, "but I dinnae want to be in the way." She was sitting beside Iain. Tyra nodded.

When Tyra entered the chamber, Sorcha's contractions came closer together, and Sorcha was in immense pain. Bram refused to leave her side. His presence calmed Sorcha, so Amelia let him stay.

And so it was, Henderson Keep settled in for a long and worrying night ahead. Each time a shout of pain or low moan could be heard from the chamber, the Keep tensed. Within the room, Amelia, Zala, and Tyra fought to keep both mother and child alive. At different intervals, Clarissa and Yesenda also lent a hand. Then just as the hour passed midnight, a loud scream reverberated off the Keep walls, then there was dead silence from within the chamber.

The men remained on tenterhooks outside. No one moved as they waited and held their breath, straining to hear. Seconds passed, and still nothing. Then there was murmuring and raised voices and finally the soft cry of a newborn bairn.

The chamber door opened several moments later, and Bram emerged, haggard and elated. His eyes were wet, then he shouted, "I have a son! Cináed Darroch Henderson because he is born of fire and strong as oak!"

The men erupted in cheers as they greeted Bram with congratulations.

Sorcha wept and held her son close to her chest while Amelia cut and tied the cord inside the chamber. She then helped Sorcha deliver the afterbirth. Ever the teacher, Amelia said, "Tyra, tis important nothing of the bairn remains inside lest it causes fever or worse."

When all was done, Zala took the babe to clean, and she wrapped him in cloth and plaid while Amelia, Tyra, and Clarissa attended to Sorcha. Within the hour, the bedding was changed, and the room was cleaned.

Sorcha was exhausted but elated as she held Cináed, now swaddled in cloths. Bram sat beside her, one arm about her shoulders as he gazed at their son.

"Hello, mo laochain," Sorcha whispered to her babe.

"Aye, he is a wee hero indeed," Bram said with pride.

The women decided to leave the couple alone so they could bond with their son. When they emerged from the chamber exhausted and weary, their husbands waited and whisked them away with haste.

Tyra waved them off, and she was surprised to see Lachlan waiting by the stairs for her. "Come, tis time for bed. You are exhausted," he said. Lachlan pulled her into his arms as they walked down the stairs. When they reached his floor, she was practically dead on her feet. Before she knew it, Lachlan lifted her into his arms and continued walking.

"Put me down, Lachie, I am too heavy."

He ignored her, and she was too tired to argue. Tyra rested her head on Lachlan's shoulder as they walked down another hallway.

"Where are we going?"

"To my room."

"But I—"

"Tis too far to your cottage, and I dinnae want you to sleep anywhere else tonight. My chamber is clean and warm."

When they walked in, Tyra noticed the bed was made, and there was a small tub by the fire with steaming hot water rising from it.

Lachlan placed her on her feet.

"The Keep staff prepared a hot bath and some clean garments. You just delivered the laird's son. They were happy to do it. I will give you time to bathe then I will return." He left the room.

Tyra stripped off and groaned when she sat in the tub. It was warm and cleansing. She scrubbed herself and dried off, then changed into a clean shift.

Lachlan knocked and entered. He removed the tub. When he returned, Tyra was in bed and fast asleep. He smiled as that warmth hit his chest again. A feeling of possessiveness stole over him that she was there in his bed, and he was determined she would remain there forever. Lachlan pulled the blanket up over her, then he washed, changed his clothes, and with his plaid, he set up a pallet on the floor by the bed.

Chapter 8

My Love

It was around 2.am when Tyra woke. She was slightly disoriented, then she remembered she was in Lachlan's room. Tyra felt well-rested even though she had slept only a couple of hours. There was a flickering candle in the corner of the room, illuminating enough light so she could see. Tyra noticed Lachlan was asleep on the floor beside the bed, and she felt terrible that his large frame must be uncomfortable in the crowded spot on the floor.

Tyra got out of bed and crouched down, tapping Lachlan's arm.

"Lachie, wake up."

He was instantly awake and sat up. "Tyra? Is something wrong?"

"No, I am hale, but I think you should sleep in your bed, and I can sleep on the pallet."

"No, tis all right I dinnae mind."

"But I do, you dinnae look comfortable, and you need your rest."

"Tyra, tis all right; go back to bed."

She remained silent for a moment, then Tyra said, "What if we both sleep in your bed? Tis big enough for two."

"No, I dare not risk it."

"What if I promise not to ravish you in your sleep?" Tyra joked.

Lachlan started chuckling. "I cannot trust you not to steal my virtue."

Tyra grinned and replied, "I swear on my honor you will leave the bed in the morning untouched."

"All right then, get back in bed, and I'll join you."

Tyra got into bed and pulled up the cover while Lachlan walked around to the other side.

It was when Tyra glanced up to watch Lachlan get into the bed that she gasped in wonder. He was shirtless, and his plaid hung low. Although the lighting was dim, it was enough to see his impressive physique. Tyra bit her bottom lip to stop from groaning. She suddenly felt as if the room was getting hotter as the blood rushed to her cheeks.

Her subtle glances did not go unnoticed by Lachlan. There was enough light for him to see every one of her reactions, and he was undone.

"Dinnae look at me that way if you wish to leave this bed untouched," he growled.

Whether it was the feeling of exhilaration having witnessed new life enter the world, or the fact that she had wanted Lachlan for so long, Tyra openly flirted back.

"Mayhap, you need to put your breeks on, Lachlan, or you will be the one who will not leave this bed untouched."

Tyra gave him her back as she turned on her side, determined to ignore him. She heard a growl and yelped when the blanket was pulled off her.

She turned back to stare at Lachlan, and he was breathing heavily; his gaze bore into her soul.

"Do you mean that, Tyra? Would you welcome my touch if I offered it now? Because I want to feel every inch of you."

Tyra nodded. "Aye, I want nothing more than to feel your hands on me, but only if you want it too."

Lachlan kept his eyes on her and slowly unwrapped his plaid. He let it drop to the floor so Tyra could see the evidence of his desire. It was standing erect for the whole world to see.

"Do you ken how much I want you now?"

"Lachie," Tyra gasped.

"Tyra, if we do this, you are mine. So, I will ask you once more. Do you want to remain untouched tonight?"

She shook her head, sat up, and said, "No, now come to bed."

"Aye," Lachlan said as he slowly crawled into bed before Tyra could change her mind. He pushed her gently back down, so she was on her back, and he hovered above her.

The only thing between them now was the flimsy shift she currently wore.

"You're beautiful, lass, so bonnie," he rasped as his lips came crashing down on hers.

Lachlan was lost in the wonder of finally having the woman he wanted in his arms. Her lips were soft against his, and he deepened the embrace as his hands roamed.

Tyra groaned and pulled away to gasp for air. Then she paused. "Wait, what about your woman? The one you were going to tell me about in the hall. Tis not right for us to do this if she is—"

"Wheesht love, my woman is right here. I am staring right at her," he whispered against her mouth.

She relaxed.

Lachlan nipped her lips with his teeth, then growled, "You have too many clothes on."

"Tis just a thin shift," she replied.

"Tis still too much. I want to feel your skin. Lift your arms," he demanded.

Tyra did as requested while Lachlan pulled the flimsy gown over her head and threw it on the ground. He gazed down at her body, and his hands traced the contour of her shape.

He thought her breathtaking, from the voluptuous breasts with stiffened peaks to her narrow waist that flared out. He took his fill as his eyes raked her body all the way to the trimmed triangular patch between her thighs.

"Lachie, please touch me," Tyra pleaded. Her hands rested on his bare chest.

Lachlan stared deep into her eyes as the candlelight flickered, providing an erotic backdrop for what they were about to do. He kissed Tyra slowly, tracing his lips down the contours of her neck. He moved down to her chest, held her ample breasts, and pushed them together. Then he lowered his head, flicked out his tongue, and licked both nipples at the same time.

"Argh," Tyra moaned as her breathing came in short bursts. And still, Lachlan's onslaught continued. He swirled his tongue across her stiffened peaks then suckled them.

Tyra felt a shot of pleasure from her breasts to her core and bit her lips to keep from moaning louder.

Lachlan took his fill as he lavished attention on her nipples. He was so aroused by her moans of pleasure; he knew she was the type of woman who could come from this alone, but he wanted more. He wanted to be buried deep inside her the first time she came with him.

Lachlan continued licking a path to her belly until his mouth hovered above her core. He pushed her knees apart, found her hooded pearl, and dove in with his tongue.

Tyra almost came off the bed.

Hearing her whimpers of pleasure almost made Lachlan cum. He was hard as a rock. He needed to stop; he needed to be inside her because he was too close to hold back. He lapped her glistening folds several times before moving back up Tyra's body. As he did, Tyra reached down and firmly gripped and caressed his length.

"No, I willna last if you do that," he pleaded.

"Tis my turn to repay the favor."

She pushed him over onto his back and captured his lips with an open-mouthed kiss. Tyra then trailed kisses down the length of Lachlan's body. Her hand remained on his shaft, rubbing up and down.

Lachlan was a slave to her passion. He groaned, and his breathing became erratic as he watched Tyra move lower. Her mouth hovered above his groin. She was staring right at him when her tongue shot out, and she licked the underside of his length from root to tip.

"Steady lass!" he hissed.

Tyra grinned, then twirled her tongue around his tip and suckled. Lachlan gripped the sheets and focused on not exploding. He stared down as Tyra set to work, pleasuring him with her succulent mouth. Lachlan watched his length disappear as she swallowed him whole.

He gritted his teeth and gently nudged her away. "No, m'eudail, please, I willna last, and I want to be inside you when I find my release."

She made a startled cry as Lachlan pulled her up.

"Ride me," he snarled.

Tyra did not hesitate; she straddled Lachlan's hips, caressed his length, and placed him at her entrance.

"That's it, mo leannan," Lachlan said. "Take me."

Tyra slowly sank down, impaling herself on his shaft. She felt every throbbing and pulsating inch of Lachlan sliding inside her. Tyra already felt full but still had a way to go. She panicked slightly. "Lachie, you are too big. I dinnae think you will fit," she said breathlessly.

He growled, "No, you will take all of me. Breathe and calm yourself. Just feel me, love."

His hand moved between them as his thumb sought out the pleasure point of her molten core. Lachlan began rubbing furiously as he continued to push his way inside, demanding she take more of him. He lifted his head and suckled a nipple. It had the required effect creating the slick lubrication needed. Tyra sank down lower until Lachlan was fully seated inside her. Her eyes glazed over with the sheer feeling of fullness and erotic pleasure.

Lachlan rasped, "That's it, love. I want you to ken who owns every inch of you."

He gripped her hips and began to thrust upwards.

"Aye, Lachie," Tyra moaned as he filled her, withdrawing and surging back in.

"Place your hands on my chest and lean forward."

She did as told, and then Tyra rode astride with abandon. Lachlan gripped her breasts with both hands while his thumbs continued to circle against her nipples before he began thrusting harder. Tyra matched his movements. She threw her head back and enjoyed the ride.

Lachlan groaned loudly as he tried to catch his breath. He had never experienced anything so visceral in his life. He gazed up at the beauty he was claiming. Her breasts bounced with each thrust as she took her pleasure. She was a vision, and Lachlan's senses were filled with only Tyra. From her dimpled cheeks to her slick wet heat, he desired every inch of her.

He almost burst every time her sheath gripped his length. But he needed more, and he needed her to come before he erupted.

Lachlan sat up and spun her onto her back, never losing connection. He gripped her knees and pushed them further apart, giving him greater access for his ultimate invasion. Tyra moaned with pleasure as Lachlan held her pinned to the mattress while he pounded hard and deep.

Tyra gripped his forearms and hung on.

They were both panting as loud moans escaped their lips.

"Watch us, sweeting. Where we are connected, look down. Watch me claiming you, mo ghràidh."

Tyra glanced down, and it was the most erotic thing she had ever seen.

She gasped, "Oh, Lachie, tis very wicked to watch."

But she could not look away as Lachlan's long thick glistening shaft slowly thrust in and out of her heat. She saw every ridge and pulsating vein as he made love to her.

Lachlan was also mesmerized by the sight of their coupling. He felt aroused, performing for her eyes only. He was slowly losing control as he watched her tight glistening centre stretched wide to engulf his length then retract as he pulled out. His blood was scorching hot with the visual display.

"Do you not think tis wicked?" she whispered and half moaned.

"I think tis beautiful, for I am claiming the woman I love. You...are...mine!" he said between thrusts.

Tyra glanced up and was struck by the truth reflected in his eyes. She lifted her head and captured his lips with a searing kiss. That was all it took for them to pick up speed and momentum.

Lachlan groaned as he pounded harder and faster, and Tyra felt something detonate inside her. She screamed as her orgasm hit. Her sheath contracted around his length, gripping him like a vice as she shuddered.

Lachlan yelled incoherent endearments as he stiffened with the sensation. He plunged deep and erupted inside her, coming so hard he could barely breathe.

When they had reached their peak, they collapsed into each other's arms, breathless and weightless, physically and emotionally satisfied beyond measure.

They fell asleep cocooned around one another, comfortable in the knowledge they would be together forever.

The Leave Taking

TWO DAYS LATER, EVERYONE was in the bailey where the men waited an extra hour while the most prolonged leave-taking in history took place between the MacGregors and their hosts. The Henderson children and MacGregor children took an age to say their goodbyes as they had all formed strong bonds playing around the Keep together. Then the MacGregor women and Henderson women took an even longer time to do as Beiste put it, "Whatever it is womenfolk suddenly find they need to do before they leave any place."

They hugged Sorcha and baby Cináed at least a dozen times and cried over missing her already. Sorcha was an emotional wreck, partly due to hormones but primarily due to her sisters fussing over her.

Bram hovered a few paces behind; however, after another round of the women mollycoddling his son, he stepped in and removed Cináed from the circle, complaining they were smothering him to death.

Beiste, Brodie, Dalziel, and their retainers kept a wide berth as well. Each held a toddler in their arms while waiting on their womenfolk and older children to finish saying their goodbyes.

Niall and Iain stood beside them.

"Bloody hell, what the devil can they have to talk about now?" Niall grimaced as he watched the simultaneous high-pitched chatter going on.

"Tis as if they have not just spent an entire month together," Iain said.

"I never ken what they're blathering on about. I just nod my head and say, 'Aye love' if I hear my name mentioned," Dalziel replied.

Brodie said, "Aye, I once made the mistake of trying to join in while they nattered, and I nearly got my head bit off. Tis a frightful thing when women gather to talk."

"Do they ever take a breath?" Iain asked.

"I can only speak for my wife, and I can tell you now, Amie can talk underwater. She does not need air," Beiste replied, and the men started chuckling.

"I heard that Beiste MacGregor!" Amelia shouted as all conversation ceased, and the women glared at Beiste.

"Blast that hearing of hers," Beiste muttered and stared at some imaginary point in the sky. Dalziel and Brodie stared at the ground, their shoulders shaking as they tried to stifle their laughter.

Iain and Niall just grinned.

Meanwhile, in female natter's inner sanctum, Amelia gave last-minute instructions to all and sundry.

"Now, mind you read my notes, Tyra, if you have any troubles with salves. You ken what I said about sundew tis good for bairns. And remember a wee bit of rose and honey to help seal wounds but clean the wound first, so no dirt is trapped inside to fester."

"Thank you, Amelia; I will keep your notes close."

"Sorcha, be sure to mind what you eat, so it does not upset the bairn through your milk. I've given Cook instructions for a rich bone broth with greens. Try to get some milk and cheese into you as well and some bread for your strength."

"Make sure everyone in the kitchen washes their hands if they mean to prepare any food for you," Clarissa said.

Zala added, "And dinnae take the bairn out when the night is cold, and the air is damp. He still needs to build up his breathing strength. You must keep his chest warm."

Sorcha replied, "I will, thank you, sisters."

The women were quiet; then, before Amelia started tearing up, she hugged Sorcha again. That started the others off, and soon the women were sniffling and crying.

Tyra, Willa, Fia, and Yesenda stepped back to give the MacGregor women some privacy.

Tyra envied their closeness, considering none were related by blood; their bond was one of the strongest she had ever seen.

When the MacGregor women were alone, Zala whispered, "Sorcha, about Lachlan and Tyra, I just want to reassure you that Heather is no longer a problem."

"You did not kill her, did you?" Sorcha asked, shocked.

"Are you daft? No, I did not kill her. I meant she has agreed to stay away from Lachlan once I told her twas all a misunderstanding."

"Oh, I see."

Zala just shook her head and turned to Clarissa, saying, "Honestly, you kill a couple of people trying to defend yourself, and everyone assumes you do it for just any old reason."

Clarissa grinned.

Then Amelia whispered, "Sorcha, I think tis working between Tyra and Lachlan. I ken she spent a night in his chamber."

"I also happened to overhear Brodie and Dalziel talking about Lachlan. They said he has been looking to acquire land so he can settle with a new bride," Clarissa said.

"Happen to overhear? Ris, you were hiding in the cupboard so you could listen in. Brodie told me he heard you sneeze," Zala said.

The women then burst out laughing while still wiping away tears.

Having lost all patience, the MacGregor men waded in to extract their wives.

"Amie, we will visit again soon, save some gossip for next time," Beiste said.

"Zala, tis time to go. We need to be on the road before the sun sets," Brodie grumbled.

"Ris, the bairns are growing restless. We best leave before they set something else on fire," Dalziel growled.

It took another twenty minutes before the MacGregors finally bade farewell and rode away from the Keep.

As she watched the group move further away, Tyra had that unsettling feeling again, that someone was watching her. She scanned the bushland area but saw nothing. Tyra shook off the feeling and returned to the Keep with the others. She made a mental note to keep her dirk in easy reach at all times.

Tyra blushed when she walked past Lachlan. He was standing at the entrance to the Keep talking to a guardsman. His eyes softened when he saw her before he turned his attention back to the guardsman. They had spent no time together since that first night. With pressing duties to attend to, there had been no time to reconnect. When they saw each other in public, they acted as expected, not wanting to draw attention to themselves, biding their time until they could be together again. Neither believed anything could ruin their blossoming affair.

They were wrong.

Chapter 9

Stolen Kisses

Later that day, Tyra was striding down the hallway when a hand reached out and pulled her inside one of the empty chambers.

She was about to scream when she heard, "Tis just me, love."

"Lachie! You scared the hell out of me," she hissed.

"Sorry, mo leannan, I've been dying to hold you, and I miss you," he said before caging her against the wall.

"You're lucky I did not stab you with my dirk."

Lachlan grinned. "You're such a spitfire and so passionate."

Tyra finally calmed and placed her hands on his chest. "You've missed me? Truly?" she whispered.

"Aye, I have. My very soul feels lost when I dinnae see you."

She rolled her eyes. "Dinnae woo me with honeyed words."

"Tis true. I have not stopped thinking about our night together. I want to feel your naked skin against mine." He kissed her neck. "I want to feel these in my hands." His hands roamed under her tunic, and he caressed her breasts.

Tyra's breathing became erratic. Then Lachlan moved forward and pressed his groin against hers. She felt the evidence of his arousal when he said, "I want to be buried deep inside you." He bit her ear lobe. "I want to feel your sheath shudder while you take me."

He leaned forward and brushed his lips against hers.

Tyra wound her arms around his neck and deepened the kiss as they writhed against the wall.

Lachlan eventually broke the kiss and rested his forehead against hers. "But most of all, I want to make you mine forever." He then framed her face with his hands and said, "I'll come to your cottage tonight. We will talk about our future and..."

"And?"

"We will do other things." He kissed her again then stepped away. He gave her a warm smile, said, "Tonight," and snuck back out into the hallway.

Tyra touched her lips, still feeling the tingling feeling of his caresses. Then she smiled and left the chamber.

High Stakes and Heartache

JUST BEFORE NOON, TYRA made her way to the weavers' room when her niece Mysie came running up to her.

"What is it, love?"

"Have you seen Aunt Sorcha?"

"No, why do you ask?"

"I wanted to play with the babe, but she is not in the solar."

"Did you check the nursery on the top floor? She is usually there around noon."

"Och, I forgot to check there, thank you," Mysie replied as she took off running.

Tyra continued to the weaving room. She heard laughter and chatter, but when she entered, the women immediately quietened down.

She heard whispers as they eyed her with curious glances.

"Good Morn," Tyra greeted them.

They nodded.

Tyra set up her workspace and noticed Blair kept looking at her as if she wanted to say something.

"Is something amiss, Blair? Did you want to ask me something?"

"Aye, Tyra, are you courting that braw Lachlan?"

Tyra blushed and replied, "I dinnae ken why that is anyone's concern, but no." She sat down and set about threading her needle.

"Are you sure about that?" Blair asked again.

The women gave furtive glances to one another.

"Aye, I am."

There was silence again as Tyra tried to ignore them all and their speculation.

"Blair is asking because she saw the two of you in the hallway earlier today, and we want to ken whether there was any stock to the rumors," Esme said.

Tyra sighed. "What rumors?"

"About the wager," Blair replied.

Tyra paused, threading her needle, and asked, "What wager?"

Several women tsked and shook their heads. Tyra looked about the circle as their expressions turned to one of pity.

Esme asked, "You really dinnae ken?"

"No. What wager?"

"That bloody Dermid, he is such a trickster!" Esme huffed.

"What has this got to do with Dermid?" Tyra asked.

Blair replied, "I heard from my Tamhas he was there that night at the Inn, and he swears that Lachlan made a wager with Dermid after they had a huge row."

Tyra was already feeling her hand shaking. "Wha... what did he wager?"

Blair hesitated then replied, "That he could bed you before Dermid did."

Tyra felt the blood drain from her face. An acute sense of betrayal and humiliation assailed her. She felt like she was going to be sick. Then she recalled Dermid trying to woo her in the cottage and Lachlan's response. It felt as if her heart was shattering into a thousand different pieces. *Lachlan bedded her to win a wager.*

Tyra stood. She was unsteady on her feet, but she needed to get away from the pitying looks directed at her. "Thank you, Blair and Esme. I assure you there was no harm done. If you will excuse me, I just remembered I have something to do."

Tyra quit the room. She could already feel the tears on her cheek as she wiped them away. Tyra had to find out for herself if this was true. She needed to give Lachlan the benefit of the doubt. *Could it all be a lie?* Urgency gave flight to her feet, and she started running towards the one place she knew she would find Lachlan, and that was the training grounds.

When Tyra arrived, she paused to catch her breath and scanned the area to find Lachlan. Her eyes rested on him by the water pails. Lachlan was shirtless and drinking water from a scoop while others milled around.

Tyra made her approach and fought the panic inside. She was determined to hear the truth from him. As Tyra strode towards him, she was about to yell his name when Dermid appeared beside Lachlan. She moved a little closer to hear what they were talking about.

Sceats

"WHAT DO YOU WANT?" Lachlan asked as he took a large gulp of water from a scoop. He had been sparring for over an hour, and he was perspiring with sweat.

"Calm doon, Gair. I came to give you these," Dermid replied.

Lachlan looked down as Dermid held something out to him. He opened his palm. Three sceats fell into his hand.

"What is this?"

"For the wager. You won fair and square."

"I dinnae want it, take it back," Lachlan replied with a scowl.

"I canna take it back. A deal is a deal. Tis rumored she spent a night in your chamber, so I take it the bargain is sealed. You bedded her before I even had a chance."

"Are you daft, Dermid? There was no wa—"

"Lachie? Is it true? Did you wager that you could bed me?"

Lachlan turned to face Tyra and stopped breathing. Her face said it all. *Devastation.*

"Tis not what it looks like, love, I swear it. I did no such thing."

Tyra looked down at the coins still in his hand. "Then what are those?"

Lachlan glanced at his hand and threw the coins on the ground. He shook his head, starting to panic. "Twas a stupid foolhardy thing, but I forgot about it, I was drunk and—"

Tyra just shook her head and started backing away. Then the tears started falling.

"*Mo ghràidh*, please..." Lachlan moved towards her.

Tyra put her hand up, warning him away. "Dinnae come near me," she yelled.

He replied, "*Mo chridhe*, no, you have to believe me, I would never do that, you ken?"

"But you did," she whispered.

Lachlan moved towards her again, and Tyra pulled out her dirk and pointed it at him. "So help me, Lachlan, if you ever come near me again, I'll cut your heart out!" she screamed.

Lachlan raised his hands palm up and said, "Please dinnae fash. Let's go talk somewhere private. I can explain, Tyra."

"Does everybody ken? Was this all part of the game?" Tyra shouted.

There was silence. She saw Kieran nearby and asked, "Did you ken, Kieran?"

Kieran looked guilty then replied, "Tyra, c'mon lass tis not like that."

Tyra deflated in disappointment. She turned back to Lachlan. "I am so stupid. You were always so cold to me, and suddenly you were nice. I thought maybe you had forgiven me, but it was all about revenge."

Lachlan took a step closer, and Tyra waved the dirk higher to stop him.

"Dammit, Tyra! Are you going to let me speak, or are you just going to the point that thing at me and keep crying?"

"I am going to bloody well point this thing at you and keep crying, you bastard!" she shouted.

"*Mo leannan*, I love you, and it is not because of some blasted wager. I ken you're angry now, but when you calm down, *we* are going to discuss *our* wedding plans because I am going to marry you!" Lachlan growled.

"Tis not that easy, Lachie, I honestly thought... I loved you. But now I dinnae trust you. I hope the sceats were worth it." With those words, Tyra turned on her heels and ran.

"Tyra! Wait!" Lachlan shouted and started after her. He got about five steps before Iain Henderson blocked his path.

"You bedded my sister? You sleekit bastard!" Iain bellowed before he pulled his arm back and with his clenched fist, he punched Lachlan right in the face.

As Lachlan hit the ground, his one hope was that the siblings let him get a word in sometime in the future.

Hell, Hath no Fury

TYRA WAS LIVID AND emotionally spent. Her eyes were swollen from bawling, and she felt humiliated in front of the entire Keep. She stormed back down the pathway and headed back to the longhouse. She wanted to put as much distance between her and Lachlan. She decided she would just work at the longhouse and stay away from the Keep.

She was almost at the glen when she heard a twig snap. The feeling of being watched assailed her again. Tyra scanned the woods and kept moving. She gripped the handle of the dirk tighter and silently berated herself for not paying attention to her surroundings. She had been distraught, but that was no excuse for dropping her guard.

"Who goes there? Show yourself!" she yelled.

There was no response. Tyra took a deep breath, silently counted to three, and sprinted toward her cottage. That was all it took for the unknown watcher to reveal himself because, in the next instant, Tyra heard the rustling of leaves and the telltale signs of someone giving chase.

A rasping voice shouted, "Miriam!"

She dared not look back or question why he called her that lest she break her stride. Instead, Tyra surged forward and kept running. She made it past the woody pathway and calmed a little, knowing there was always a guardsman milling about in that area. But when she arrived, there was no guardsman in the usual place. She was still trying to deal with that fault in her plan when she tripped and went flying, hitting the ground hard. Tyra rolled over to see what tripped her, and she stared straight into the guardsman's dead eyes. His throat was slit.

She screamed and scrambled on all fours, panic urging her to get back on her feet and keep running. Her dirk now lay a foot away, dropped when she tumbled. She felt someone right behind her. Tyra lunged for the blade, then screamed when someone grabbed her hair and pulled her backward. She fought like a wildcat, trying to get him to release her. Then she was on her back, staring straight up at a stranger, a man with deep blue eyes. His hand still gripped her hair.

"You are not Miriam. Where the hell is Miriam?" he roared.

"I dinnae ken any Miriam."

"Fucking liar."

Tyra shuddered in fear when he pulled out a knife and aimed it at her head. He flicked it around in his hand before he struck. The last thing Tyra saw was the dagger's handle aiming straight for her temple before everything went black.

Fist Fights

BACK AT THE TRAINING grounds, another battle was raging.

"I'm going to beat you to a pulp for ruining my sister!" Iain shouted as he came at Lachlan again with fists flying.

"I didnae ruin her if you would just listen to me!" Lachlan yelled, trying to dodge the fists and kicking Iain in the shin.

"So you're saying she was already ruined?" Iain landed a punch right under Lachlan's chin.

Lachlan returned the favor with a jab to the ribs before he pushed Iain away. "I said no such thing, you daft prick!"

"Fuck you!" Iain replied, planting two quick hits to Lachlan's jaw.

Lachlan roared and punched Iain in the rib cage. Iain was priming to pummel him some more, but Lachlan was not having a bar of it. He stepped to the side and ran at Iain, knocking him to the ground.

Iain bellowed in outrage, and it was on for young and old as the two men grappled in the dirt.

"All right, that's enough!" Bram Henderson yelled. "You have made a spectacle of yourselves long enough. Not to mention dragged Tyra's good name through the mud, airing all your secrets for the world to hear."

Bram grabbed Iain and pulled him away as Kieran pulled Lachlan away.

They realized then a large crowd had gathered.

"You both need to walk away and calm down," Bram demanded. Then he turned to Iain and said, "I need you to check on Sorcha and my son while I see to other matters."

Iain grunted, nodded, and stormed away.

Lachlan shook Kieran off him, picked up his sword, and started walking out of the Keep, still shirtless.

"Where are you going now?" Kieran asked.

"To find Tyra and talk some bloody sense into that woman."

Kieran shook his head and said, "Good luck."

The Riverbank

WHEN TYRA CAME TO, she was shivering with cold and lying on the riverbank. The damp soil was seeping through her bones. Her head ached from the hit, and she was slightly groggy. But she tried to focus on her surroundings.

She pretended to be unconscious when she heard footsteps nearby and murmuring conversation. She felt around her and found a jagged-edged rock; she grabbed it and clutched it tight in her hand. She caught a glimpse of two men. One wore pilgrim garb, the other wore a brown robe with a cross. Their hair was cut peculiarly, and from their speech, they were Normans. She knew they were most likely part of a religious order. *Clerics*, she thought.

"She's not Miriam," the one who attacked her said.

"Then Miriam must be in the Keep. There is a way to get to her."

"What do you want me to do with this one?"

"Kill her."

"Are you sure?"

"Aye. But hide the body well; we cannot have people alerted just yet."

Tyra stiffened with fear. She knew she had to try and do something, but she waited for the right moment.

"I'll meet you back at the Inn when the deed is done."

Tyra remained still. She worked through all the scenarios in her head of what she needed to do to survive.

When the cleric turned back towards her, Tyra lay still and feigned sleep.

He approached and stood over her, talking to himself. "Tis a pity I have to kill you. You're a pretty one, that's for sure. I think I'll drown you."

He picked her up, and that's when Tyra struck. She said, "I think not," then struck him on the side of the head with the jagged-edged rock.

The cleric dropped her with a stunned expression on his face. The blood was trickling down the side of his face. Tyra rolled onto her feet and scrambled up the ravine. Shaking his head several times to stop the dizziness, her attacker unsheathed his blade and ran after her. Tyra stumbled and lost her footing. She slid back down the ravine. It was a crucial error because the cleric was already on her, his dagger raised.

He aimed for her face, but she moved her head to the side as the blade sank deep into her shoulder. Tyra screamed and struggled to push him off her. He withdrew the knife and lifted it up to stab her again. Tyra grabbed his wrist to stop the downward momentum, but she knew it was futile.

As her entire life flashed before her eyes, her last thought was that she wished she had given Lachlan a chance to explain himself. The blade came down again, she moved, and this time it sliced her arm. He raised his arm again, aiming straight for her heart. Tyra blocked it with her forearm. She grabbed his wrist with both hands, trying to stop the blade from piercing her chest.

"You should not have hit me. I would have given you a peaceful death," he said.

He put more weight and pressure on the blade, knowing that eventually, Tyra would have to let it sink into her heart.

Tyra could feel her strength waning as the blade inched ever closer to her chest. She was losing blood as it seeped into the ground. Like the mighty Samson and the pillars of the Temple of Dagon, Tyra sent a prayer for just enough strength to hold a little longer. She pushed back as hard as she could and closed her eyes, accepting the inevitable.

Tyra opened her eyes when she heard running footsteps followed by a bellowing roar, "Get off her!"

In an instant, the cleric was gone, the blade was gone, the pressure gone, and Tyra heard the clash of steel. She turned her head to the side as she watched two men battle with swords. She whispered, "Lachie," then passed out.

She's a Mystery Girl

IAIN HENDERSON WAS fuming. If Bram had not interrupted him, he would have loved nothing more than to pummel Lachlan Gair until there was nothing left of him. He was primed for a good fight and was annoyed the opportunity was stolen from him.

Lately, Iain had been feeling out of sorts. Liosa was messing with his head again, and things had changed between them. Or maybe he was just changing. In the past, he would have bent over backward to please her; now, he just felt a distance he could not explain.

"I am getting too old for this shite," he muttered to himself as he climbed the steps to the first floor of the Keep where the family stayed. Bram was now seeing to crofters, and he had asked Iain to check on Sorcha and the bairn. Iain trudged up the steps, feeling bone-weary and tired. He had been feeling weary about life in general lately. The only bright spot in his day apart from his niece and nephews was someone entirely unexpected. Yesenda MacDonald had breezed into his life like a gale-force wind. Even the thought of her had him grinning to himself.

Iain frowned when he wondered why her brother Ruadh thought she attracted trouble. Iain had spent enough time with Yesenda to know she was too quiet to cause any concern. His inner thoughts were interrupted when he heard a woman urgently whisper, "Iain!"

He stilled and looked around.

"Up here," she said.

Iain stared up at the ceiling, and his heart lodged in his throat. Yesenda MacDonald was balanced and propped up on the high corner of the wall adjacent to the large Drawing Room. No one inside would see her, but she had a clear view. Her left foot rested on one wall, and her right rested on the other. She wore trews, a tunic, and a cloak. One hand gripped the wall to maintain balance; the other hand made a 'Sh' signal in front of her face. Then she pointed at the large room ahead and mouthed, "Sorcha. Mysie."

Iain instantly reached for his claymore and made his way quietly towards the door.

"Iain!" she whispered again.

He whipped his head up when she mouthed, "You stay. I go."

Iain ignored her and stepped closer to the Drawing Room. There was a second entrance through an old stairwell that had since been boarded up. But it could be reached via the rafters. Iain peeked through a crack, and his blood ran cold.

Sorcha was on her knees, her hands tied behind her back. A guardsman lay unconscious just inside the doorway. When he looked beyond the guardsman, he saw why Sorcha was not moving or shouting for help even though he knew she could fight off any attacker. It was because a terrified Mysie held baby Cináed in her arms while a pilgrim pointed a spiked head war club at her. One hit from it could kill them both. Iain knew Sorcha was at a disadvantage, and she would not risk losing the children.

"I will ask you again. Where is Miriam Ferguson?" the pilgrim demanded.

"I am telling you, we dinnae ken who she is!" Sorcha replied, exasperated. "Please let them go. They are just bairns." Her voice was shaking with emotion.

Iain knew the only way to save them was to find a way inside the room so he could distract the pilgrim long enough for the others to escape. He glanced up to signal to Yesenda that he was going in, but the blasted woman was gone. He had not even heard her move. Iain's only thought was, *What the hell?*

Chapter 10

Mysterious Miriam

"You will tell me where Miriam Ferguson is, or I will kill the babe."

"No! Please, I beg of you. I speak the truth. We dinnae ken who Miriam is," Sorcha said.

Mysie was trembling as she clutched her little cousin. Her eyes widened in fear when the pilgrim replied, "Then I will kill the girl."

It was then Yesenda slowly stepped out of the shadows and said, *"Relinquam illam solam. Ego hic."* – Leave her alone, I am here.

The pilgrim replied, *"Miriam, ego expectavimus diu."* – I've waited a long time.

Sorcha and Mysie stared at Yesenda in confusion but dared not move.

Yesenda took a step closer and said, "When did you become such a coward that you would quarrel with bairns? Let them go. I have what you want."

The pilgrim scoffed, "You think me foolish? I know what you are. I will not make it past the door unless I have the babe as safe passage."

Yesenda focused on the spiked war club he wielded. He waved it above Mysie's head as he spoke. Without taking her eyes off the pilgrim, Yesenda said in a calm voice, "Mysie, dinnae drop your cousin. Hold him tight."

Mysie sniffled, nodded, and held him a little closer to her chest.

Yesenda then addressed the pilgrim, "If you leave the bairns alone, I will come with you unarmed. I have what you seek. We can both leave in one piece."

The pilgrim contemplated her offer.

Yesenda could just make out Iain hovering beyond the door. She waited for Iain to do what she assumed he would. Then she could do what she was trained to do.

As the seconds ticked by, Iain finally stepped into the room, and when he did, his shoe hit a creaky floorboard, giving away his position instantly. That was what Yesenda was waiting for. Trust a man not to do what he's told, she thought.

Then she moved.

With bare feet as swift as Hermes, son of Zeus, Yesenda sprinted towards the pilgrim while Iain's entrance momentarily distracted him. She reached under her cloak and pulled out her weapon.

"Run, Mysie!" she yelled. Mysie ran.

The pilgrim swung his spiked war club, aiming at the children, but instead of piercing flesh, it clashed against Yesenda's eight-flanged bronze head mace. She wielded it with such force, the pilgrim staggered back slightly.

"Brother Mateo has taught you well," he grunted.

Yesenda did not reply but kept her attention on the pilgrim as they slowly circled one another. From the corner of her eye, she could see Iain freeing Sorcha so she could get the children to safety.

The pilgrim said, "You know Brother Mateo used to be one of us? And then he grew soft. He traded immortality for a bunch of useless women!" He swung his club again, this time aiming for her head. He was strong and adept at his weapon. So was Yesenda. She dodged the hit, expertly rotated her mace in her right hand, and blocked the crushing blow. Time and again he swung, and Yesenda parried each hit while she pivoted from side to side.

"You have a strong right hand, but you'll need to do better than that to kill me," the pilgrim said, laughing.

"Where the bloody hell did you get that thing?" Iain growled as he entered the affray with his claymore.

"A lady never tells," Yesenda replied.

"What on earth are they teaching at the abbey nowadays?" Iain muttered as he narrowly missed a blow to the head.

"You'd be surprised," Yesenda replied.

"Get down!" Iain yelled. Yesenda ducked as Iain blocked the club with his claymore.

"Move!" Yesenda shouted, and Iain sidestepped as Yesenda swung her mace with her right hand at the pilgrim's left side to hinder him.

The pilgrim switched his war club to his left hand and expertly blocked her attack. He chuckled. "Surprise! I am trained to combat with both hands. That's the problem with you right-handed women. You cannot match my skill." He dodged Iain's blade and ran at Yesenda so fast. It almost took her by surprise. Almost.

The pilgrim aimed his war club at her right hand to dislodge her weapon. In a move he hadn't anticipated, Yesenda flicked her mace behind her back. It twirled high into the air. While her eyes remained on the pilgrim, she raised her left hand and caught the handle of her mace. She rotated it with all her might and brought it crashing down against his unguarded rib. It connected, and she heard the crunching sound as the flanges broke bones and tore through his flesh.

The pilgrim winced in pain as shock registered on his face.

As he collapsed to his knees, Yesenda said, "'Tis lucky that I am actually left-handed."

The pilgrim still attempted to swing his club. Iain slammed his foot on the handle and kicked it away. The pilgrim grimaced in pain as blood poured from his wound. His breathing was shallow, and Yesenda was familiar with the sound. It was from broken ribs and a punctured lung. If she did not help him soon, he would die.

"Who sent you?" Yesenda demanded.

He remained silent.

"Tell me who sent you, and I can heal your wounds," Yesenda said.

Still, he remained silent.

"Answer her!" Iain shouted.

The pilgrim stared at Yesenda, his face a mask of unsettling serenity. He pulled out a dagger and yelled, *"Nam Episcopus et Anglia!"* — For the Bishop and England. Then he stabbed himself in the heart.

"No!" Yesenda shouted. But it was too late as the pilgrim fell forward, dead.

"What the devil is going on, Yesenda? Why did he call you Miriam?" Iain asked.

At that moment, Bram came bursting through the door with Sorcha close behind. "What is happening? Who is this man, and why did he try to murder Mysie and my bairn?"

"Calm down, Bram, let her speak. She just saved our lives," Sorcha said, clearly recovered from her ordeal.

"I dinnae have time to explain. All I ken is if he is here, danger lurks close by. Are the bairns safe?" Yesenda asked Sorcha.

"Aye, Niall and Fia are with them now," Sorcha replied.

"What do you mean, the danger is still close by?" Bram asked.

Yesenda replied, "This man is part of a brotherhood. They travel in twos, and one is never far from the other. Wherever they travel, people end up dead. Alert the guards and keep your family close."

"Why did he call you Miriam?" Iain asked again.

"I dinnae ken. I just played along to give me time," Yesenda lied.

Iain gave her a skeptical look but said nothing.

Yesenda asked Sorcha, "Did he mention anything else, anything of importance that you might have thought strange?"

"Aye, he said something about healers."

"Where is Tyra?" Yesenda asked.

"She was headed back to the glen the last I saw her," Bram replied.

"Then she is in danger." Yesenda bolted for the door.

"Where do you think you're going?" Iain shouted as he sprinted after her.

Heal the Healer

TYRA AWOKE. SHE WAS bleeding out, and she could feel the cold sickness seeping in. Her body was losing heat. She tried to sit up but had no strength. Her one consolation was seeing the dead cleric's body lying by the river and Lachlan's sword stained with blood.

Lachlan ran to her, the look of worry clearly expressed on his face as he stared at the blood. He picked her up and held her close to his chest. "Tyra, stay with me, sweeting," he pleaded as he started running towards the longhouse. Tyra's teeth were chattering, and her lips were turning blue. Her eyes rolled to the back of her head, and she passed out again.

As Lachlan made his way up the path to the longhouse, he ran into the others. The look of fear on his face was palpable. Soon they moved in unison to rally around Tyra.

Iain and Bram paled when they saw the deathly pallor of their sister and cousin. They exchanged quick words of explanation. Bram and his men went to retrieve the bodies of the cleric and the murdered guard. Iain rode back to the Keep, fetching Willa and Sorcha so they could help Tyra. Yesenda ran straight ahead to the longhouse.

Lachlan burst into the longhouse with Tyra in his arms. He was thankful there was a fire going with hot water on the boil. There were also blankets and towels.

Yesenda quickly cleared the table and said, "Lay her there. We need to get the wet clothes off her. You can stand outside while I—"

"No!" Lachlan replied. "I will stay and help you."

"But her modesty—"

Tyra lay shivering in Lachlan's arms and near exhaustion. Seeing her that way unmanned him.

"Please. I canna leave her," Lachlan pleaded, his voice guttural and filled with emotion.

"Aye, alright, put her down now," Yesenda said.

Together they stripped her of her wet clothes. Lachlan wrapped her in a warm plaid while Yesenda carefully cleaned the wounds to her shoulder and her arm.

"The shoulder wound is deep. Tyra will lose more blood if I dinnae close it. The cut on her arm should only require a bandage," she said.

"Do you need a hot blade to close the flesh?" Lachlan asked.

"No, I ken something better. Press this cloth against Tyra's shoulder while I gather some things."

Lachlan pressed a clean cloth against the wound and waited for Yesenda. Yesenda moved about the cottage, gathering things. When she returned, she had catgut sheep thread and a needle. She washed her hands, threaded the needle, then poured hot water on both.

"Hold her steady while I sew."

Lachlan nodded and kept Tyra still. Then he watched in awe as Yesenda's deft fingers made neat stitches along Tyra's skin.

"Where did you learn to do this?" he asked.

"In the abbey. The nuns teach us their ways."

Willa and Sorcha arrived with Iain. Willa made up a clean bed with warm blankets for Tyra to convalesce. She also cooked up a bone broth. Sorcha helped Yesenda treat and bandage the wounds.

Iain stepped inside and threw a clean shirt at Lachlan. "The least you can do is put some bloody clothes on!" He scowled then walked back outside.

Lachlan realized he had been shirtless the whole time since the training grounds. He quickly donned the léine. The women took turns cleaning Tyra and drying her hair so she did not catch a chill.

Eventually, they settled Tyra on Lachlan's lap close to the fire because she called for him. Lachlan did not object.

Iain came back inside and gritted his teeth at the sight of Lachlan cradling his sister, but he said nothing.

"Will she be all right?" Iain asked.

"We need to watch her for fever, but if the wound does not fester, she should be well," Yesenda replied, and Sorcha agreed.

There was movement at the door, and Liosa entered. "Iain, I was just at the Keep. I was so afraid for you. I heard there had been an attack. Are you well, my love?" Liosa asked as she fussed over Iain.

Iain was slightly embarrassed but assured her he was all right and advised that she return to Willa's old cottage. Willa and Sorcha gave Liosa filthy glares when she left, but Yesenda just smirked.

"What are you smirking at?" Iain asked as he made to leave.

"I just thought of some timely advice for you, Warrior."

"And what's that?"

"Be careful where you sheath your claymore," she replied.

Iain flinched, shocked by Yesenda's comment. He opened his mouth to say something, then shut it again. Then he threw his head back and burst out laughing.

Yesenda just grinned and went back to her task.

An hour later, Tyra was sleeping peacefully against Lachlan's chest, and her lips were less blue. The color was returning to her cheeks. Lachlan dozed in the chair, his arms firmly around her until he felt Willa tap him on the shoulder.

"Lachlan, she can rest now in her bed. Lay her there, then you can find your rest too," Willa said, giving him a warm smile.

Lachlan stood and carried Tyra to bed. He gently laid her down and then moved out of the way as the women fussed over her and covered her with thick bedding.

Sorcha said, "Lachlan, there's hot water left over. You can have a warm wash in the other room. Then come and join Tyra. You need to watch her tonight in case of fever."

"Aye, I will do it," he replied, grateful that they were letting him spend time with her.

Eventually, Sorcha and Willa returned to the Keep with Bram.

Yesenda remained in Tyra's cottage if needed, and after a welcome warm bath and change of clothes, Lachlan settled in beside Tyra.

Her Protector

LACHLAN ADDED ANOTHER log to the fire then got back into bed beside Tyra. He felt her forehead, and although it was a little clammy, there was no sign of fever. Needing to be closer, he gently pulled her body against his, draping one arm over her stomach. He pushed a lock of hair away from her face and breathed a sigh of contentment. She almost died and would have if he had not arrived in time. He shuddered when he recalled seeing the cleric attempting to kill her. As soon as Tyra was better, they would need to talk about their future. There was no way he was ever going to let her go. Those were his last thoughts as he drifted off to sleep.

Just before dawn, Tyra woke to a roaring fire. She lay naked, tucked under a warm fur cover. She felt so toasty and comfortable despite the niggling pain in her shoulder and arm. She turned to see where she was, coming up against a hard-muscled wall.

An arm tightened around her. "Dinnae even think of getting out of this bed," Lachlan said.

Tyra blushed when she realized he was in bed with her. Then she remembered the events of the previous day.

"Lachie, is everyone safe? There was another man headed to the Keep."

"Dinnae fash, all is well." Lachlan pulled her closer and kissed her forehead.

"Where are the others? How come you are here?" she asked, still slightly confused and sore.

"The others are resting elsewhere. I promised to remain with you and watch for fever."

He felt her forehead again with the back of his hand. "Are you hale? How do you feel?"

"A little sore, but I am well. Does Iain ken you are here?" she whispered.

"Aye."

"And he allowed it?"

"Aye."

Tyra suddenly felt exhausted. She snuggled back into his embrace and closed her eyes. Resting her head on his shoulder, she kissed his chest then snuggled again.

Lachlan held her tight in his arms and said, "Go back to sleep, sweeting. We will talk in the morn."

She smiled and drifted off to sleep.

Slàinte Mhath

LACHLAN FELT SOMEONE shaking him awake. He reached for his sword when Iain said, "Settle down, 'tis just me."

He extracted himself from Tyra and tucked her under the blankets then sat up.

"What is it?" he asked Iain. Lachlan noticed it was pre-dawn outside.

Iain just glared at him then pulled up a chair by the fire. He still did not speak.

Lachlan sighed, rose from the bed, and pulled up a chair on the opposite side of the table.

"You saved Tyra's life," Iain said.

"Aye."

"I thank you."

"No thanks necessary. I would die for Tyra."

"What happens now?" Iain asked.

"What do you mean?"

"You've spent the entire night with my sister in the longhouse with no one else about. Soon word will spread. So, I will ask you again, Gair, what happens now?"

"I am going to marry her," Lachlan replied.

"Aye, you will. I dinnae like you, but I ken Tyra needs you."

Iain rose, grabbed two cups and a bottle of whiskey. He poured two serves, sat, and gave one to Lachlan. "Drink," he said.

Lachlan lifted the cup and said, "*Slàinte Mhath.*"

Iain lifted his cup and replied, "*Do dheagh shlàinte.*"

Both men made eye contact, skulled the dram, and placed their cups on the table.

Iain stood and headed for the door. When he opened it, he paused and said over his shoulder, "If you hurt her in any way, Lachlan, I will slit your throat in your sleep. I've done it before. Welcome to the family." With those parting words, Iain left.

Lachlan exhaled the breath he didn't realize he was holding and just shook his head. Then he looked over at the bed and watched Tyra sleeping, oblivious that her life was about to change. He gazed upon her lovingly and felt joy and hope explode in his chest. She was his now, and that feeling alone warmed his heart.

The following morning, after Lachlan washed in the river and changed into fresh clothes, he returned to the longhouse to help Tyra bathe. Her shoulder was stiff, and she was still sore from the previous day's ordeal. She was currently sitting in a large tub filled with warm water, rinsing off the soap.

"Lachie, I look a sight."

"You're bonnie to me, love."

Tyra blushed and turned away.

He held her chin and turned her to face him. "Dinnae turn from me. 'Tis true. You are the bonniest woman in the entire world. No other compares to you. Even when we're in our dotage and the young-uns call us old and grey, you'll still be the bonniest lass in the Highlands."

Tyra leaned across and brushed her lips against his. "Thank you for saying that."

Lachlan grinned, then helped her out of the bath. He wrapped her in a large drying cloth and pulled her onto his lap by the fire, where he proceeded to dry her hair.

Chapter 11

Frustration

It was two weeks after the ordeal, and Tyra was out of sorts. She had recovered remarkably well thanks to Yesenda's healing care. But it seemed Lachlan was avoiding her. She had not seen him for days and wondered if maybe he had lost interest. She ran through all the possible scenarios in her head, and none of them felt good.

Sorcha assured her Heather had left Glencoe. Kieran explained the full details of the wager which put her mind at ease. But she worried about the woman she saw leaving his room. She told Yesenda about it, and Yesenda confessed that she had walked into the wrong chamber by mistake. The other women assured her that Lachlan was just busy with urgent matters, so she tried to remain calm.

Then her heart plummeted when she heard from Bram that Lachlan had left for Glenorchy. Feeling dejected and hurt, Tyra decided it was time to protect her heart. Instead of heading to the Keep for a noonday meal, Tyra remained in her little cottage and sulked. She busied herself pottering around, and she resolved never to speak of Lachlan ever again.

Lost in her sulking, she felt a presence hovering close by and knew who it was. Lachlan stood in her doorway, casually leaning against the door frame.

"Tyra."

"Aye," Tyra replied and continued to stir the mixture. She refused to pay him any more attention.

"I was in Glenorchy."

"I heard," she said and moved to hang some cloth by the fireplace.

"Are you not curious why I went there?" he asked.

"Not really."

Lachlan gritted his teeth, then stepped inside the cottage and slammed the door.

"Dinnae break my door, Lachlan, there's a cold evening coming, and I prefer not to have a draft," she snapped.

"Lachie!" he growled.

She looked at him, confused. "What do you mean?"

"Lachie, you will call me Lachie."

She snorted, then resumed her chores and said, "I will do no such thing, Mr. Gair." She emphasized the formality of his title then turned her back to him to reach for a jar by the bench. Tyra did not get very far. One minute she was standing by the fireplace, and the next, she yelped in surprise as Lachlan had her over his shoulder as he walked towards the bed.

"Put me down!" she yelled.

"With pleasure," he replied and tossed her onto the bed, being careful of her shoulder. He followed her down, effectively hovering above her. Their faces were inches apart as he held his weight off her and balanced on his elbows. His eyes were soft, and he just kept staring at her.

Tyra glared back. "Get off me!" she demanded, but he would not budge.

"Not until you say my name, lass."

She huffed and pursed her lips tighter in defiance.

"Stubborn wench," he muttered.

Lachlan refused to move, but his mouth curved upwards into a smile.

Tyra continued to glare at him while he began caressing her face gently with the back of his hand, causing her to feel a plethora of emotions. She shivered when he gently caressed her neck. His hand moved lower into dangerous territory.

"All right. Get off me, Lachlan Gair."

"No. You ken 'tis not what I want." He casually stroked the curve of her hip.

"Fine then. Lachie, please get off me."

Lachlan grinned and paused. "Repeat my name, love."

"Lachie," she said with a slight huskiness to her voice.

His entire face lit up into a wide grin. Tyra had a hard time catching her breath. He indeed was a handsome man when he smiled. It was the most beautiful thing she had ever seen.

Lachlan immediately got up and helped her off the bed. "That was not so hard, was it?" he asked with a raised eyebrow.

Tyra shook her head and made to move away, then found herself on his lap as he sat down on a chair.

"What now?" she said in a curt tone.

"Now, we are going to talk. I'm going to talk, and you will listen."

"How—"

Lachlan placed a finger on her lips to stop her words. "You will listen first, then you can scream like a banshee later. Nod if you ken what I mean?"

Tyra scowled at him but nodded.

He removed his finger and pulled her closer. "I came to tell you I will move in here tomorrow."

"Why?"

"Because we are getting married tomorrow in a chapel on Henderson land with close friends and family in attendance. There will be a wedding breakfast afterward, which is already arranged."

She opened her mouth to protest when he stopped her again.

"I went to Glenorchy to gather all my belongings and notify my chieftain that I will not be returning. He gave me his blessing."

Tyra opened her mouth to speak, but Lachlan stood abruptly, placed her on her feet, and covered her protests with his lips. He ended the kiss and whispered, "I'll see you tomorrow. Sorcha and Willa will be here in the morn to help you get ready for our wedding."

Lachlan opened the door and quit the cottage, leaving a stunned, flustered Tyra wondering what the hell just happened. Then she shouted out the window, "That is the worst offer of marriage I have ever heard!"

She could hear Lachlan chuckling outside.

Bonds of Love

"THAT'S IT, TYRA, JUST like that. Take me deeper," Lachlan groaned as he watched Tyra above him, riding him with abandon. He was caressing her breasts as he thrust his engorged length upward into her welcome heat. Tyra threw her head back as she moaned in ecstasy. She covered one of his hands with hers while the other rested on his chest for balance.

A feeling of deep possessiveness and satisfaction stole over Lachlan as he watched the light reflect off the gold wedding band on her ring finger and the matching one on his. Then he felt her entire body stiffen and shudder as she found her peak.

Tyra shouted, "Lachie!" and made a high-pitched keening sound.

Watching his wife find her pleasure was the most erotic thing Lachlan had ever seen. As her core gripped him harder, he exploded inside her with a roar. Tyra collapsed onto Lachlan's chest and, as her eyes bored into his soul, he captured her lips with his, sealing their love once more.

As they lay together in the afterglow, Lachlan smiled, recalling their perfect wedding, hours earlier. It comprised a small chapel service attended by close family and friends. Kieran stood by his side as best man, and Willa by Tyra's side. An exchange of vows and rings symbolized their love and fidelity. The wedding breakfast included simple fare, with an abundance of food for everyone. The ceremony and feast were what the bride and groom wanted, with some sweet treats for the children afterward. For a last-minute wedding, it was as if the couple had planned it themselves weeks ago.

Epilogue

Henderson Keep, Glencoe, Scotland

One Month Later

"Where will you go now?" a deep masculine voice asked.

Yesenda turned to see Iain casually leaning against the wall in the hallway.

"I have a friend in Normandy I need to see and another in England," she replied.

"Is it safe to go alone?"

"As safe as any other place, I suppose," Yesenda replied.

"How do you ken that?" Iain walked towards her; a concerned look furrowed his brow.

"'Tis just what I heard. If you will excuse me, I have things to do before I leave."

Yesenda tried to bypass Iain, but his arm shot out, and he gently but firmly pulled her back towards him.

"Dinnae lie to me, lass, are you in danger? Is that why you are leaving?" Iain asked.

"We're all in danger, Iain. If you love your clan, you will understand why I cannot stay. Trouble follows me wherever I go. I will not endanger the people I love."

They stared at one another for some time, then Iain nodded and released her arm.

Yesenda let out the breath she did not realize she was holding. Thinking he excused her, she walked toward the stairs when instead, she found her hand clasped firmly in Iain's as he pulled her down the hallway.

"What are you doing?" she asked as she tried to tug her hand free, but he only tightened his grip.

Iain replied, "I am going to find out what this danger is, and you, my lovely Yesenda, are coming with me."

The End

Up next is Iain & Yesenda's story in 'Highland Warrior.'
For more details, visit https://elinaemerald.com[1]

---

1. https://elinaemerald.com/books

Also by Elina Emerald

Cambridge
Lucas
Victor: Cambridge Book 2

FRIVEN EMPIRE
The Eleventh House: A Sci-fi Romance
The Vedora Key: A Sci-fi Romance
The Dead of Winter: A Sci-fi Romance

Keeper of Secrets
Highland Warrior: Keeper of Secrets
Highland Guard

Reformed Rogues
Betrothed to the Beast
Betrothed to the Beast
Handfasted to the Bear
Pledged to the Wolf

The MacGregors
Arrowsmith
Sorcha
Lachlan

Standalone
Reformed Rogues plus Arrowsmith Book Bundle
Highlander Undone
His Runaway Bride
To Tame a Viking Warlord

Watch for more at https://elinaemerald.com/books.

9 798201 504380